Shadows

&

Illumination

Unveiling the world struggle
between truth and deception

Gabriel Garang Pioth

The publisher wishes to acknowledge and thank Dr. Douglas H. Johnson for his invaluable help and support for Africa World Books and its mission of preserving and promoting African cultural and literary traditions and history. Dr. Johnson and fellow historians have been instrumental in ensuring that African people remain connected to their past and their identity. Africa World Books is proud to carry on this mission.

ISBN: 9780645819526

Cover design, typesetting and layout: Africa World Books
Unit 3, 57 Frobisher St, Osborne Park, WA 6017
P.O. Box 1106 Osborne Park, WA 6916

This book is dedicated to the fearless seekers of truth.

Dedication

This book is a testament to the unwavering determination of those, who delve into the depths of deception to unearth the essence of truth. To those who tirelessly unravel the enigmatic dance between light and darkness, weaving a tapestry of understanding that illuminates the world's struggles. To my family, who stood by my side through the obscure paths of discovery, shedding light on the darkest corners of my endeavours, your unwavering support and love have been the beacon that guided me through the labyrinth of knowledge. To my friends, who challenged my perceptions and enriched my journey with their diverse perspectives, your conversations sparked the flames of curiosity that ignited this exploration into the interplay of shadows and illumination. To the mentors and teachers, whose wisdom and guidance served as a compass in deciphering the complex symphony of truth and deception, your illuminating lessons have etched a lasting mark on my quest for understanding. To the strangers who crossed my path, their stories cast light and shadows upon me. Each encounter has contributed to the puzzle of the world's enigmatic struggle. To the written words, the melodies, and the strokes of art that have illuminated my mind and soul in moments of obscurity, your presence has been a source of solace and inspiration as I unveiled the layers of truth hidden within the shadows. The relentless pursuit of truth is the driving force behind this endeavour. You revealed the profound interplay between shadows and illumination, guiding my pen on this journey. I dedicate this book to all who embrace the deep struggle between truth and deception. May its words resonate with your quest and strengthen your resolve to confront the shadows and illuminate the world with truth.

With heartfelt dedication,
Gabriel Garang Pioth

Table of Contents

The Beginning

In a world shrouded in enigmatic depths and intricacies, the perpetual battle between truth and deception rages on, an ever-present tempest that demands an unwavering commitment to discerning reality from illusion. This timeless conflict takes on multifaceted guises, permeating the very fabric of our existence, from the tumultuous realm of politics to the manipulative realm of media, from the intricate tapestry of personal relationships to the labyrinthine corridors of our minds.

Within the pages of this captivating tome, titled "Shadows and Illumination: Unveiling the World Struggle between Truth and Deception," we embark on an exhilarating and contemplative odyssey, delving deep into the eternal clash between deception and truth. Deception and truth are used interchangeably with shadow and illumination, respectively. Let it be clear from the outset that the names of people and places mentioned in this book are ideal, and perfect utopia places/names that can exist anywhere in the world. They are not historically grounded in ideal conditions describe in this book. This book strives to inspire the power dynamics at play by drawing upon the annals of history, untangling the intricacies of psychological insights, and illuminating our understanding with poignant contemporary examples. The book aspires to ignite a fiery passion within its readers, encouraging them to rise as champions of truth.

In a world where the landscape is increasingly shaped by the ebb and flow of information and disinformation, grasping the nuanced nuances of this monumental struggle becomes an imperative quest. By unraveling the enigma that veils truth, this book seeks to empower individuals, equipping them with the necessary tools to traverse the treacherous terrain of deception. It beckons readers to recognize their role in shaping a more enlightened future, where the beacon of truth shines unyieldingly, casting its light upon the shadows of falsehood and deceit. The fascinating question that begs for an answer is how did deception come to dominate our world.

The evolution of deception is a fascinating aspect of animal behavior that has developed over millions of years[1]. Deception refers to deliberately manipulating information or signals to mislead others, with the aim of gaining an advantage in various contexts such as predation, competition for resources, and reproduction. It is observed across multiple species, from insects to mammals, including humans. For instance, organisms that possess traits allowing them to deceive others in their environment gain a selective advantage by increasing their chances of survival and reproduction. As a result, deceptive behaviors tend to become more prevalent and refined over time. Similarly, some prey animals have evolved deceptive strategies to avoid being detected by predators. The classic example are the behaviors of the praying mantis and chameleon, which use camouflage and motionless mimicry to blend into its surroundings and ambush unsuspecting prey.

On the other hand, predators have evolved deceptive tactics to increase their hunting success. Some species, like angler fish, possess a modified dorsal fin that acts as a lure, attracting prey towards their waiting jaws. Some birds of prey, may exhibit "mobbing" behavior, pretending to be injured or vulnerable to attract potential threats away from their nest or young ones. Deception or deceit is also observed in social interactions and reproductive strategies. Male birds may engage in deceptive displays, exaggerating their physical traits or mimicking the songs of high-quality individuals to attract mates. Female fireflies emit misleading light signals, mimicking the flash patterns of other species to lure unsuspecting males closer.

In the case of humans, deception has played a significant role in our evolutionary history. As social beings, we have developed complex cognitive abilities that enable sophisticated forms of deception. This includes lying, bluffing, and strategically manipulating information to achieve personal or social goals. It is therefore fair to say that the evolution of deception is an adaptive strategy that has emerged across different species. It has evolved because of selective pressures and serves various functions, such as enhancing survival, improving reproductive success, and gaining competitive advantages. The examples mentioned here are just but a few illustrations of the diverse ways deception has evolved in nature.

Let us define the truth. As a profound and timeless concept, truth encompasses a multifaceted essence that resonates with accuracy, honesty, and sincerity at its core. It serves as an unwavering compass, guiding us toward unraveling the authentic nature of events, ideas, and individuals. Embracing truth empowers us to pierce through the veil of deception and biases, enabling us to perceive the world. The illumination or light is used in place of truth in this book.

In its magnificent significance, truth is the cornerstone of knowledge and understanding. It forms the bedrock upon which the edifice of human intellect is constructed, fostering a realm where ideas can be examined, evaluated, and expanded upon. By seeking truth, humanity embarks on an unending journey of discovery and enlightenment, constantly evolving our comprehension of our universe.

Moreover, truth catalyzes the prosperity of societies, providing them with a stable and dependable foundation. Its presence within the fabric of human interactions cultivates trust, fostering genuine connections and promoting harmonious relationships. When truth prevails, individuals are bound by a shared understanding, nurturing social cohesion and enabling communities to flourish.

Equally crucial is truth's profound impact on justice. It

serves as a guiding principle, illuminating the path toward equitable outcomes and ensuring fairness prevails. With truth as the compass, judgments are made based on facts rather than assumptions or biases, reinforcing the principles of righteousness and preventing the erosion of fundamental rights. Truth acts as a judge, resolving disputes and upholding the principles of integrity and accountability.

Beyond its role in knowledge, society, and justice, truth also emboldens progress. It acts as a catalyst, propelling us forward by challenging existing paradigms and illuminating previously hidden paths. By embracing truth, we empower ourselves to question, innovate, and refine our understanding of the world, opening doors to groundbreaking advancements in science, technology, arts, and every facet of human endeavor.

However, truth does not exist in isolation; it exists in a constant struggle with its formidable adversary, deception. Deception, a cunning and elusive force, thrives on a web of falsehoods, intricate manipulation, and clever distortion. Deception can assume various guises like a chameleon, ranging from blatant propaganda and insidious misinformation to the artful use of subtle half-truths and brazenly crafted lies. Its insidious purpose is to sow seeds of doubt, mislead the unsuspecting, control the vulnerable, and exploit the gullible. Motivated by personal gain, the hunger for dominance, or the insatiable thirst for power, deception weaves its complex drapery of falsehoods, leaving unsuspecting victims entangled in its illusions. It preys upon the human propensity for trust, undermining the foundations of honesty and integrity and leaving a trail of confusion, disillusionment, and shattered realities in its wake. The battle between truth and deception is a perpetual struggle that requires constant vigilance, critical thinking, and an unwavering commitment to unraveling the tangled threads of deceit to uncover the elusive truths that lie beneath. Only through the pursuit of knowledge, the quest for transparency, and the unwavering dedication to unraveling the intricate web of deception can we hope to illuminate the path toward a more enlightened and honest world.

In today's interconnected world, the struggle between truth and deception has reached unprecedented heights, propelled by the rapid advancement of technology and the widespread presence of social media. These developments have ushered in a new era where the dissemination of information has become democratized, enabling individuals to share their perspectives and opinions more freely than ever before. However, this freedom has come at a cost, as it has also given rise to an alarming surge in misinformation and disinformation. False narratives now have the potential to spread like wildfire, fueled by the power of online networks and further amplified by echo chambers—groups of like-minded individuals who reinforce and validate one another's beliefs, often with little regard for integrity. Moreover, algorithms employed by various platforms often prioritize user engagement over the accuracy of the information, creating an environment where sensationalism and clickbait thrive. At the same time, reliable sources struggle to be heard.

Consequently, the battle to discern truth from falsehood

has become increasingly arduous, requiring individuals to navigate a maze of conflicting narratives and deliberate distortions. In this complex landscape, it has become crucial for individuals to cultivate critical thinking skills, fact-check information from multiple sources, and remain vigilant against the seductive allure of misinformation. Only through a concerted effort to promote media literacy, transparency, and responsible online behavior can we mitigate the detrimental effects of this era of information warfare and restore trust in the pursuit of truth.

In this ongoing struggle, truth frequently finds itself in an unfavorable position, pitted against the formidable deception forces. The art of deception possesses an unsettling power, employing persuasive and emotionally compelling tactics and deftly exploiting humanity's vulnerabilities. Through the clever manipulation of people's deepest fears, ingrained biases, and insatiable desires, falsehoods gain a foothold in the minds of individuals, creating a web of confusion and distortion.

In contrast, truth is a beacon of intellectual integrity and honest discourse, but its path is riddled with obstacles. Pursuing truth demands a willingness to embrace complexity and appreciate nuance, for it seldom exists in oversimplified narratives or soundbites. Unraveling the threads of truth requires an active engagement with critical thinking and a commitment to diligent fact-checking, as it often hides within a maze of competing perspectives and subjective interpretations.

However, the struggle to unearth truth becomes even more

arduous in an era characterized by the relentless deluge of information. The modern landscape inundates individuals with a ceaseless barrage of contradictory messages, competing narratives, and distorted claims. This overwhelming influx further complicates the already daunting task of discerning the veracity of statements and distinguishing truth from falsehood. Amid this cacophony, the search for truth demands unwavering vigilance, the ability to sift through the noise, and an unyielding dedication to seeking reliable sources and corroborating evidence.

Yet, despite its disadvantages, truth remains an enduring ideal, a steadfast foundation upon which the pillars of knowledge and understanding are constructed. It is the driving force behind progress, justice, and human enlightenment. Though its path may be treacherous and riddled with obstacles, pursuing truth remains an essential endeavor deserving our collective commitment and unwavering determination. We aim to uncover the facts that shape our world and empower us to make informed decisions by overcoming the challenges posed by deception, navigating the complexities of information, and embracing critical thinking.

The consequences of this battle are profound. Societies polarize, public trust erodes, and the very fabric of democratic institutions weakens. When truth is undermined, decision-making becomes flawed, policies are based on lies, and individuals are susceptible to manipulation. The struggle between truth and deception can result in dire outcomes, from eroding civil liberties to perpetuating injustice and inequality.

Yet, amid the chaos, the pursuit of truth remains essential

and should be won. It requires an informed and engaged citizenry, a commitment to critical thinking, and a willingness to question authority. It demands media literacy, fact-checking, and responsible journalism. It necessitates the courage to challenge our own biases and preconceptions. Addressing the pervasive influence of deception necessitates a concerted and collaborative endeavor. Governments, institutions, and individuals must commit to transparency, accountability, and disseminating accurate information. There are several ways to pursue truth in our society.

Governments must enact policies prioritizing openness and transparency to combat the prevalence of deception. By fostering an environment of accountability, governments can establish mechanisms to ensure the accuracy and integrity of information disseminated to the public. Legislation mandating transparency in political campaigns, public service announcements, and official communications can be crucial safeguards against deceptive practices.

Institutions, including corporations, non-profit organizations, and educational establishments, are responsible for upholding ethical standards in their operations. Internal processes that encourage honesty, integrity, and openness can mitigate deception. Moreover, these institutions can actively promote educational initiatives to enhance media literacy, critical thinking skills, and digital citizenship. By empowering individuals to discern accurate information from falsehoods, institutions can foster a society more resilient to deception's influence.

At the individual level, each person has a role in combating deception. Individuals must prioritize seeking out reliable sources of information and questioning the veracity of claims before accepting them as truth. Engaging in critical thinking, fact-checking, and being mindful of biases can help individuals navigate the sea of misinformation. Additionally, individuals should actively support and engage with reputable fact-checking organizations that hold public figures and institutions accountable for spreading falsehoods.

As vital gatekeepers of truth, fact-checking organizations play a pivotal role in countering deception. These organizations employ rigorous methodologies to verify the accuracy of claims made by individuals, institutions, and the media. By providing impartial evaluations and evidence-based analyses, fact-checkers equip the public with the tools to make informed decisions and challenge deceptive narratives.

Education initiatives are paramount in cultivating a society that values truth and accuracy. Educational institutions should incorporate media literacy programs into their curricula, teaching students to analyze information and identify misinformation critically. Equipping future generations with the skills necessary to discern fact from fiction will enable them to participate actively in a society that prioritizes truth.

Ethical journalism plays a central role in restoring faith in the media and countering deception. Journalists are responsible for reporting the news with accuracy, integrity, and objectivity. Adhering to ethical standards, such as verifying sources, fact-checking claims, and avoiding sensationalism, is crucial in combating deception. Encouraging investigative journalism and supporting independent media outlets can also diversify sources of information and promote a plurality of perspectives.

Ultimately, the struggle between truth and deception is not a fleeting or temporary conflict; instead, it is an ongoing, perpetual battle that continuously challenges the resilience and integrity of societies. This enduring struggle serves as a litmus test for the strength and character of individuals, communities, and nations.

In this age-old battle, truth is the beacon of light, the fundamental pillar upon which justice, enlightenment, and authenticity are built. It is a guiding principle that illuminates the path toward a better world. The triumph of truth signifies a victory over the forces of falsehood, deceit, and manipulation that seek to undermine the very foundations of a just and enlightened society.

We must hold an unwavering commitment to truth to engage in this battle. It demands our wholehearted dedication to seeking and embracing the truth in all our lives. We must be willing to challenge our preconceived notions, question established narratives, and scrutinize information with a discerning eye. By doing so, we can rise above the allure of deception and strengthen our capacity to discern fact from fiction.

The struggle between truth and deception is not a solitary endeavor but a collective responsibility. It necessitates the active participation and collaboration of individuals, communities, and institutions. Promoting transparency, accountability, and open dialogue can create an environment where truth can thrive. Through honest and authentic interactions, we can foster mutual understanding, empathy, and trust, thus building solid foundations for a just and harmonious society.

However, this battle has its challenges. Deception, in its various forms, can be insidious, pervasive, and tempting. In an era of rapidly evolving technology and information dissemination, the propagation of misinformation and manipulation has reached unprecedented levels. Fake news, deepfakes, and disinformation campaigns have the potential to sow discord, erode trust, and fracture the social fabric. To overcome these challenges, we must equip ourselves with critical thinking skills, media literacy, and a healthy dose of skepticism. We need to develop the ability to discern reliable sources of information, verify facts, and separate truth from distortion. By nurturing a well-informed and discerning society, we can counter the influence of deception and safeguard the integrity of our shared reality.

The triumph of truth holds immense transformative power. It has the potential to dismantle oppressive systems, expose corruption, and challenge prevailing narratives. We pave the way for a more just, equitable, and compassionate world by upholding truth as the cornerstone of our societal structures.

In pursuing truth, we must recognize that it is not a static destination but a continuous journey. Our understanding of truth evolves as we gather new knowledge, engage in meaningful discourse, and expand our perspectives. It requires intellectual humility, open-mindedness, and a willingness to confront uncomfortable truths.

In conclusion, the perpetual struggle between truth and

deception is a battle that tests the resilience and integrity of societies. It demands our unwavering commitment to truth, for it is through the triumph of reality that we can hope to build a world that is just, enlightened, and guided by the principles of honesty and authenticity. Only by embracing the transformative power of truth can we collectively forge a brighter future for generations to come.

Chapter One:
The Seeds of Deception

In the opening chapter, we went over the dawn of civilization, where deception took root as a fundamental survival tactic. This chapter explores the strategies employed by early human tribes to protect themselves and gain advantage, we'll trace the roots of deception and its early manifestations in society. From the shadows of ancient politics to the rise of cunning leaders, we'll see how deception began to intertwine with power, influencing the fate of nations.

In the vast records of human history, deception has been a perennial companion, often intertwined with the human condition itself. From political machinations to personal relationships, the seeds of deception have been sown with calculated precision, altering destinies and shaping the course of nations. This intricate web of lies and deceit has profoundly impacted society, leaving a trail of shattered trust and shattered lives. Probing into the depths of this complex phenomenon, this exploration aims to shed light on the origins, mechanisms, and consequences of deception, ultimately unearthing the true nature of the seeds of deception.

1. The Nature of Deception

Deception, in its essence, is a multifaceted phenomenon that involves the intentional and strategic act of misleading others, concealing the truth, or manipulating information for personal gain, power, or advantage. It encompasses many tactics, including outright lies, half-truths, omissions, camouflage, and perception manipulation. Deception thrives in the shadows of secrecy, taking advantage of the vulnerabilities present in human cognition and emotion, thereby subverting our ability to discern truth from falsehood accurately[2].

At its core, deception is a deliberate and purposeful action driven by various motives. Individuals may use deception to protect their self-interests, maintain control or dominance over others, gain advantages in competitive situations, or avoid negative consequences. Deception always requires careful planning, strategic thinking, and understanding the target audience's beliefs, desires, and vulnerabilities. One common form of deception is the use of outright lies. Lies use creative false narratives, manipulate public opinion, or manipulate interpersonal relationships. Sometimes, lies shield one's true intentions or cover up past misdeeds.

Half-truths are another deceptive tactic frequently

employed. They reveal only a portion of the truth while omitting crucial details or context. By selectively presenting information, deceivers can shape the perception of events and steer others towards a particular interpretation that aligns with their objectives. This manipulation of truth can effectively influence opinions and decision-making processes.

Deception can also manifest through omissions, where individuals strategically withhold relevant information. By intentionally omitting key details, deceivers can create a distorted or incomplete picture of a situation, leading others to draw inaccurate conclusions. Omissions can exploit the human tendency to fill in the missing or gaps in information with assumptions or beliefs, thus perpetuating deception. In social media, people can pass you their preconceived idea or theory and urge you to pass it to more other people. If you do so without thinking properly, you have participated in perpetuating the deception schemes.

Camouflage is yet another method employed in deception, often used in the natural world but also adopted by humans. Camouflage involves blending into the surroundings or assuming a false appearance to deceive others about one's true identity, intentions, or motives. Deceivers can use camouflage to hide one's true agenda, gain trust, or create a false sense of security. As dangerous as physical camouflage in military, so is the deception camouflage.

Furthermore, deception often capitalizes on the vulnerabilities present in human cognition and emotion. Our cognitive biases, such as confirmation bias or the halo effect, can make us susceptible to manipulation and influence our ability to evaluate information critically. Additionally, emotional appeals, manipulation of fear or desire, and exploiting trust can all be tactics employed by deceivers to manipulate perceptions and distort reality.

In summary, deception is rooted in deliberately misleading others, concealing the truth, or manipulating information for personal gain, power, or advantage. It encompasses many forms, including lies, half-truths, omissions, camouflage, and perception manipulation. Deception thrives in the shadows of secrecy, exploiting vulnerabilities in human cognition and emotion, thereby subverting our ability to discern truth from falsehood. Understanding the mechanisms and tactics of deception is crucial in developing critical thinking skills and safeguarding against manipulation in various aspects of life.

2. Historical Perspectives of Deception

Throughout the records of time, the intricate fabric of human history is interwoven with the enduring presence of deception[3]. From ancient civilizations to the modern era, the seeds of deceit have been sown by those who wield power, driven by the relentless pursuit of control and dominance over their fellow beings. In the grand theatre of politics, the cunning strategies of political leaders, dictators, and demagogues have been honed to perfection, utilizing deception as a potent tool to shape public opinion, galvanize support, and subject entire populations to their will.

Across the vast expanse of centuries, empires have risen

and fallen, each leaving its indelible mark on the pages of history, often propelled by calculated acts of deception. In the courts of ancient and modern rulers, advisers and strategists concocted elaborate schemes to secure their reigns, employing artful manipulation to maintain their grip on power. Cleverly constructed narratives and carefully crafted falsehoods presented an image of strength and invincibility, concealing the true intentions and vulnerabilities beneath the surface.

As civilizations progressed, the art of deception evolved alongside them, adapting to the changing times and technological advancements. With the advent of mass communication, propaganda emerged as a potent weapon of manipulation, capable of disseminating false narratives on an unprecedented scale. Dictators and totalitarian regimes seized upon this powerful tool to orchestrate vast deception campaigns, distorting reality and subverting the truth to further their agendas. They manufactured consent through censorship, controlled media outlets, and sophisticated psychological techniques, perpetuating their rule and suppressing dissenting voices.

Even in democracies, where the ideals of transparency and accountability are held in high regard, the specter of deception has cast its shadow. Political leaders have sometimes succumbed to the allure of deceit, employing carefully worded rhetoric, half-truths, and even outright lies to sway public opinion and maintain their positions of authority. Elections, the bedrock of democratic systems, have witnessed strategic misinformation campaigns to manipulate voters and undermine the democratic process.

The consequences of deception throughout history have been profound, altering the course of nations and leaving lasting scars on societies. Wars have been waged, their origins rooted in false justifications and manufactured provocations. Revolutions have been ignited, fueled by the collective anger of populations who have awoken to the web of deceit spun around them. The rise and fall of entire civilizations have hinged upon the delicate balance between truth and falsehood, as leaders' manipulation of reality shapes the destiny of millions.

Yet, amid the darkness of deception, hope and resilience emerge. Throughout history, brave individuals, independent thinkers, and truth-seekers have fought against the tide of falsehoods, risking their lives and reputations to expose the truth and bring about change. Journalists, activists, and whistleblowers have acted as beacons of honesty, challenging the prevailing narratives and shining a light on the murky depths of deception.

As we gaze upon the mosaic of human history, we witness the pervasive influence of deception intricately woven into the fabric of our collective past. From the ancient empires that rose and fell to the modern democracies grappling with their demons, the legacy of deception is a stark reminder of the fragility of truth and the enduring struggle for transparency and authenticity. Only by acknowledging the historical perspectives of deception can we strive to build a future where the seeds of truth flourish, and the webs of deceit are exposed, fostering a society rooted in integrity, trust, and the unyielding pursuit of truth.

3. Human Psychology and Vulnerabilities

Deception frequently capitalizes on various aspects of our psychological makeup, aiming to exploit our weaknesses and steer us towards accepting false information or misguided beliefs. One crucial cognitive bias that deceivers often leverage is confirmation bias. This bias manifests when individuals actively seek out and interpret information in a way that aligns with their existing beliefs or expectations. Rather than objectively evaluating information, individuals tend to favor data that confirms what they already believe, reinforcing their preconceived notions. Deceivers capitalize on this tendency by presenting selectively chosen evidence or framing their arguments in a way that resonates with people's pre-existing beliefs, leading them further down the path of deception[4].

Emotional manipulation serves as another potent tool in the arsenal of deceivers. By exploiting our desires, fears, and hopes, they skillfully manipulate our emotions to achieve their ulterior motives[5]. Deceivers understand that when our emotions are engaged, our ability to think rationally and critically may be diminished. They leverage this vulnerability by appealing to our deepest desires, preying on our fears, or offering false promises that trigger positive emotions. By manipulating our emotions, they can control our thoughts and actions, leading us to make decisions that we might not otherwise make.

The advent of technology and the widespread use of social

media have significantly amplified the reach and impact of deception. In today's digital age, misinformation can spread rapidly and effortlessly, reaching a vast audience within seconds. Social media platforms have become breeding grounds for disseminating false information, often designed to manipulate public opinion and distort reality. Deceivers can exploit these platforms' algorithms and echo chambers, ensuring their deceptive narratives gain traction and become widely accepted.

The consequences of deception in the digital era are far-reaching. Misinformation can shape public opinion, influence political discourse, and impact essential decision-making processes. It can undermine trust in institutions, erode social cohesion, and perpetuate false narratives that are detrimental to society. Recognizing and understanding the psychology behind deception is crucial for individuals to guard against manipulation and critically evaluate information presented to them, particularly in the age of digital connectivity.

4. The Mechanics of Deception

Deception is a complex process that often involves the manipulation of cognitive biases and emotional responses, taking advantage of how our minds work. One of the critical mechanisms deceivers utilize is confirmation bias, which refers to the tendency of individuals to seek out and interpret information that confirms their existing beliefs or preferences. This cognitive bias makes people more susceptible to manipulation, as they are inclined to accept information that aligns with their preconceived notions.

Moreover, emotional manipulation plays a crucial role in the art of deception. Deceivers skilfully prey upon our desires, fears, and hopes, leveraging these powerful emotions to further their objectives. By tapping into our deepest aspirations or exploiting our insecurities, they can influence our decisions and actions, steering us toward their desired outcomes. This manipulation of emotions is a potent tool that allows deceivers to gain trust, sympathy, or compliance, ultimately facilitating the success of their deceptive endeavors[6].

In recent years, the advent of technology and the widespread use of social media platforms have significantly augmented the reach and impact of deception. With the click of a button, misinformation can spread rapidly across online networks, reaching a vast audience within seconds. This rapid dissemination of false or misleading information can distort public opinion, shape narratives, and even alter the perception of reality. The interconnectedness of individuals through social media allows for the amplification and reinforcement of deceptive messages as they are shared, liked, and commented upon by others. Social Media creates an echo chamber effect, where many people can reinforce and accept falsehoods as truth, further perpetuating the cycle of deception.

The pervasive influence of technology and social media has also provided deceivers with new avenues for manipulation. They can exploit algorithms and target specific audiences with tailored messages, enhancing the effectiveness of their deceptive campaigns. Additionally, the anonymity and anonymity afforded by the internet enable deceivers to operate with relative impunity, making it challenging to trace the source of misleading content or hold individuals accountable for their actions.

Overall, the mechanics of deception are intricate and evolving. By exploiting cognitive biases, manipulating emotions, and leveraging the power of technology and social media, deceivers can exert significant influence over individuals and society. Recognizing these mechanisms and developing critical thinking skills are essential in navigating an increasingly complex and deceptive landscape.

5. Consequences and Ethical Dilemmas

The effects of deception are far-reaching and profound. At the individual level, trust is eroded, relationships are fractured, and the fabric of society is weakened. When trust is eroded, people become wary and skeptical, making it challenging to form meaningful connections and maintain healthy interpersonal bonds. Individuals who have been deceived may experience feelings of betrayal, anger, and disillusionment, leading to emotional distress and psychological harm.

At a broader societal level, deception in the public sphere can have disastrous consequences. Public figures, leaders, or institutions engaging in deceptive practices can lead to social unrest and political instability. The revelation of deception in governmental or corporate entities can trigger public outrage and erode confidence in the systems that are meant to serve and protect society. This loss of faith in institutions can further exacerbate societal divisions, sow mistrust among citizens, and undermine the democratic process.

Furthermore, the pervasive nature of deception raises profound ethical dilemmas that challenge our moral compass and decision-making processes[6]. Deceptive acts force us to confront personal and collective responsibility questions. Is it acceptable to deceive others if it serves the greater good? Should individuals be held accountable for the consequences of their deceptive actions? These dilemmas highlight the tensions between individual autonomy and the well-being of the collective.

Deception also brings to the forefront the delicate balance between privacy and transparency. In an age of information overload and constant connectivity, individuals and organizations grapple with how much information should be shared and what should be kept hidden. Deceptive practices can infringe privacy rights, as individuals may feel pressured to reveal personal information under pretenses. On the other hand, transparency is essential for maintaining trust and accountability within society.

Moreover, the limits of acceptable behavior in pursuing personal or societal goals are challenged by deception. When individuals or groups engage in deceptive tactics to achieve their objectives, it raises ethical concerns about the means justifying the ends. It prompts us to reflect on the values and principles that should guide our actions, especially when faced with difficult choices that may involve deception.

Addressing the consequences and ethical dilemmas of deception requires a multifaceted approach. It involves fostering a culture of honesty, integrity, and transparency in both personal and public spheres. Education and awareness campaigns can help individuals recognize the potential harms of deception and the importance of building and maintaining trust. Institutions and leaders must prioritize ethical decision-making, accountability, and open communication to rebuild public trust. Additionally, ongoing discussions and debates about the boundaries of acceptable behavior can help refine our understanding of ethics in the context of deception, guiding individuals and societies toward more ethical practices[8,9].

6. Unmasking Deception

Deception's pervasive presence in human affairs may seem like an impossible challenge. However, some effective strategies and measures can be implemented to mitigate its impact and foster a more transparent and honest society. By employing critical thinking and promoting media literacy, individuals can be empowered to navigate the vast sea of information and effectively identify falsehoods and deceit[10].

One crucial approach to combating deception is through rigorous fact-checking. In an era where misinformation spreads rapidly, verifying the accuracy of claims and statements becomes essential. Fact-checking initiatives by individuals and dedicated organizations play a pivotal role in exposing falsehoods and revealing the truth. Society can establish a collective commitment to accuracy and integrity by promoting and supporting such efforts.

Transparency in governance is another vital aspect of countering deception. When governments operate with openness and accountability, it becomes harder for deception to thrive. By ensuring that decision-making processes, policy formulation, and implementation are conducted transparently, citizens gain trust in their leaders. This transparency allows for increased scrutiny and the ability to hold those in power accountable for their actions, reducing the likelihood of deception going unnoticed.

Robust legal frameworks also play a crucial role in combating deception in the public sphere. Laws explicitly addressing fraud, false advertising, and misinformation provide a framework for holding individuals and entities accountable for their deceptive practices. Establishing consequences for dishonest behavior and ensuring that legal systems have the necessary resources and expertise to investigate and prosecute such cases creates a strong deterrent, discouraging individuals and organizations from engaging in deceptive activities.

However, addressing deception goes beyond implementing external measures. Cultivating a culture that values honesty, integrity, and ethical conduct is fundamental to dismantling the foundations upon which fraud thrives. This involves instilling these values in educational systems, businesses, and society. By promoting ethics and integrity in all aspects of life, individuals are more likely to embrace honesty and reject deception as an acceptable means to an end.

In conclusion, the seeds of deception have been sown

throughout history, infiltrating various aspects of our lives. Understanding the acts' nature, mechanics, and consequences is crucial in safeguarding ourselves and our societies from its insidious effects. By cultivating a commitment to truth, transparency, and ethical conduct, we can unravel the web of lies and sow the seeds of a more honest and resilient future.

Chapter Two:
The Rise of Truth-Seekers

As civilization continued its relentless march forward, propelled by the collective yearning for progress and enlightenment, a remarkable group of individuals emerged from the depths of obscurity. These brave souls were driven by an insatiable curiosity and an unwavering dedication to piercing through the carefully woven veils of deception that had shrouded the minds of humanity for far too long.

In the enthralling chapter that lies ahead, we shall embark on a captivating journey through the accounts of history, venturing into the lives of some of the greatest philosophers, scientists, and thinkers who ever graced our world. These intellectual giants – truth seekers, driven by an indomitable spirit, fearlessly championed the cause of truth, wielding their intellect as a mighty weapon against the forces of deceit that sought to confine the human mind. "Truth Seekers" is a term commonly used to refer to individuals or groups who actively pursue the discovery of truth, often in relation to hidden knowledge, deep understanding, or uncovering concealed information. These truth seekers are driven by a strong desire to unveil the realities obscured or distorted by various forces such as misinformation, secrecy, or propaganda[11].

Our expedition commences with Socrates, a luminary whose relentless pursuit of wisdom ignited a flame illuminating the path of countless generations. Fearless and unyielding, he fearlessly questioned his time's established norms and dogmas, urging his fellow beings to introspect and embrace the profound beauty of knowledge. Socrates' unwavering commitment to truth and his steadfast desire to unlock the depths of human understanding cost his life and left an indelible symbol of intellectual courage and resilience on the world[12].

As we continue on our odyssey, we encounter the visionary brilliance of Galileo Galilei, whose unwavering quest to comprehend the vast expanses of the cosmos propelled him beyond the confines of conventional wisdom. Armed with his groundbreaking observations and daring hypotheses, Galileo fearlessly challenged the entrenched beliefs of his era, revealing the true nature of the celestial bodies and forever altering humanity's perception of the universe. Yet, his audacity came at a significant cost, as he faced severe consequences for his defiance of the prevailing orthodoxy, serving as a stark reminder of the resistance encountered by those who dared to question the status quo[13].

Finally, amidst the shadows of a world engulfed in

deception and falsehood, Nelson Mandela's unyielding spirit emerges as a beacon of illumination, illuminating the struggle between truth and deceit. Born in a land tainted by apartheid's darkness, his unwavering determination to dismantle injustice and unite his homeland shone brightly. Even as the shackles of imprisonment attempted to obscure his vision, Mandela's undying hope unveiled a path toward a united, free South Africa. His journey epitomized the battle between shadows and illumination, as he used the power of truth, justice, and forgiveness to lead his nation toward reconciliation and progress. Elected as the first black President in 1994, he cast a radiant light on the end of apartheid, revealing the transformative force of one person's courage and vision, forever leaving a legacy that inspires the world's ongoing struggle between truth and deception[14].

These towering figures were not alone in their pursuit of truth. The embroidery of history is interwoven with countless other luminaries who, against all odds, confronted the boundaries of human knowledge and the entrenched powers that sought to suppress their voices. Through their relentless curiosity and uncompromising commitment to unravelling the mysteries of existence, these truth-seekers ignited a spark of enlightenment that would transcend their lifetimes and inspire future generations to embrace the unquenchable thirst for truth.

In this chapter, we shall bear witness to the triumphs and tribulations of these extraordinary individuals as they navigated treacherous waters in their unwavering devotion to truth. Their collective endeavors laid the foundation for the intellectual and scientific progress that continues to shape our modern world, reminding us of the indomitable spirit of those who dare to challenge the boundaries of knowledge, even in the face of immense adversity.

The motivations behind the pursuit of truth are manifold and can differ significantly among individuals who identify themselves as truth seekers. People embark on this quest with varying intentions and desires, each driven by unique perspectives and values. One of the primary motivations for seeking the truth is a genuine thirst for knowledge and understanding. These individuals are driven by a deep curiosity and a hunger to resolve the world's mysteries. They seek to expand their intellectual horizons, grasp the underlying principles that govern our reality, and comprehensively understand various subjects. For them, pursuing truth is an enriching and fulfilling endeavor driven by an inherent love for learning.

Others are motivated by a sense of justice and fairness. These truth seekers are compelled by a desire to uncover and expose hidden truths that may have been suppressed or manipulated. They see truth as a powerful tool for holding individuals, institutions, and systems accountable. By bringing confidential information to light, they aim to challenge and rectify injustices and create a more equitable and transparent society. Their pursuit of truth is driven by a moral obligation to seek justice and confront deception.

Furthermore, some are motivated by a desire to challenge the status quo. They question the prevailing narratives, ideologies, and dogmas that shape society. A rebellious spirit drives these truth seekers to challenge established norms and beliefs. They believe that pursuing truth involves questioning everything, even widely accepted notions, to foster progress and encourage critical thinking. They hope to uncover alternative perspectives and possibilities by challenging the status quo, enabling a more open and dynamic society.

Regardless of their specific motivations, truth seekers share the goal of seeking clarity and uncovering the underlying truths that shape our world. They recognize that truth can be complex and elusive, requiring diligent inquiry and a willingness to confront uncomfortable realities. Pursuing truth may involve rigorous research, critical thinking, and an openness to different viewpoints. It requires intellectual humility and the recognition that truth is a process subject to revision and refinement as new information emerges.

In summary, the motivations behind the pursuit of truth are diverse and can range from a thirst for knowledge and understanding to a sense of justice and a desire to challenge the status quo. Despite these differences, truth seekers share the goal of seeking clarity and uncovering the underlying truths that shape our world. Their collective efforts contribute to a more enlightened and informed society, fostering progress, justice, and the betterment of humanity.

Truth seekers employ diverse methods and approaches in their relentless pursuit of truth. Their commitment to uncovering the truth is evident through their tireless efforts in conducting extensive research, using critical thinking skills, and meticulously analysing the available evidence. Rather than passively accepting prevailing narratives, truth seekers actively question them, recognizing that superficial or convenient explanations often fall short of comprehensive understanding. They dig into the depths of information, persistently challenging established beliefs, institutions, or ideologies that may hinder the discovery of truth.

To expand their knowledge and perspectives, truth seekers explore alternative viewpoints that offer fresh insights. They recognize the value of considering differing opinions and ideas, acknowledging that a comprehensive approach leads to a more well-rounded understanding of complex issues. In their quest for truth, truth seekers examine historical events, undertaking rigorous investigations to separate fact from fiction. They scrutinize official records, recognizing the potential for bias or manipulation, and strive to unveil hidden truths that may have been overlooked or intentionally obscured.

Furthermore, truth seekers actively seek out firsthand accounts, recognizing the power of personal experiences in shaping a more accurate understanding of the world. They value the voices of individuals who have witnessed or directly participated in significant events, acknowledging the significance of their perspectives in constructing a comprehensive narrative.

The relentless dedication of truth seekers to unravel the truth often leads them to challenge the status quo, standing up against established norms or systems that hinder genuine understanding. They approach their quest for truth with an open mind, unafraid to confront uncomfortable or unpopular ideas if they contribute to a more accurate representation of reality.

In summary, truth seekers employ many methods and approaches to unravel the world's mysteries. Through extensive research, critical thinking, and analysis, they strive to question prevailing narratives and unearth hidden truths. By exploring alternative viewpoints, investigating historical events, scrutinizing official records, and seeking firsthand accounts, truth seekers construct a more accurate and comprehensive understanding of our world.

In recent years, the advent of the digital age has revolutionized the landscape for truth seekers, enabling them to engage in their pursuit with unprecedented ease and efficiency. The rapid growth of the internet and the widespread adoption of social media platforms have ushered in a new era where information is more readily available than at any other point in human history. This accessibility has fundamentally transformed the way in which individuals seek, analyze, and disseminate knowledge. With a few clicks of a button or taps on a screen, truth seekers can access an astonishing array of information spanning various subjects and perspectives. The internet is an expansive knowledge repository, housing vast libraries, scholarly journals, reputable news outlets, and personal blogs. This immense digital library empowers individuals to explore diverse viewpoints, delve into different cultural perspectives, and expand their world understanding.

However, amidst this digital cornucopia of information lies a challenge that truth seekers must contend with the proliferation of fake news and disinformation. The same platforms that have made information more accessible have also become breeding grounds for the spread of misleading or intentionally fabricated content. The viral nature of social media, coupled with echo chambers and algorithms that reinforce preexisting beliefs, has created an environment where falsehoods can rapidly propagate and gain traction.

In this sea of information, truth seekers find themselves faced with the critical task of navigating through a complex web of sources, evaluating their reliability, and discerning fact from fiction. They must develop a keen eye for identifying credible sources, assessing the validity of claims, and cross-referencing information to ensure its accuracy. This requires honing critical thinking skills, actively questioning the origins and motivations behind the data, and seeking out diverse perspectives to gain a more comprehensive understanding.

Moreover, truth seekers must employ digital literacy skills to distinguish between reputable sources and those driven by biases, ulterior motives, or outright falsehoods. They must be mindful of the techniques used to manipulate information, such as selective editing, cherry-picking data, or emotional appeals to sway opinions. Truth seekers can better discern the nuances between reliable journalism and sensationalized or misleading narratives by equipping themselves with media literacy tools.

To thrive in the digital age, truth seekers must also understand the importance of collaboration and collective intelligence. Engaging in online communities, participating in fact-checking initiatives, and sharing knowledge with others who share a commitment to truth can bolster efforts to combat misinformation. By leveraging diverse individuals' collective wisdom and expertise, truth seekers can uncover deeper insights, challenge biases, and collectively advance the pursuit of knowledge.

In conclusion, the digital age has brought unprecedented opportunities and challenges for truth seekers. While the internet and social media platforms have made information more accessible than ever, they have also increased the proliferation of fake news and disinformation. Navigating this vast sea of information requires critical evaluation of sources, fact verification, and cultivating digital literacy skills. By leveraging the power of collaboration and collective intelligence, truth seekers can rise above the challenges and uncover the truths that lie within the digital realm.

The truth-seeking journey is a complex and arduous path that demands unwavering commitment, perseverance, intellectual rigor, and an open mind. It is a difficult road but rather a challenging and often uphill climb. Truth seekers embark on this journey with a deep desire to unravel the mysteries, uncover hidden facts, and expose the truth that lies beneath the surface.

Along the way, truth seekers encounter numerous obstacles that test their resolve. One of the most significant challenges they face is resistance from those who prefer to maintain the status quo of misinformation or secrecy. These individuals or groups may have vested interests in concealing the truth or manipulating information for personal gain. As truth seekers challenge the established narratives, they often find themselves confronted with skepticism and even hostility from these very sources.

In their pursuit of truth, these seekers may face ridicule or be unfairly labelled as conspiracy theorists. Society sometimes tends to dismiss or marginalize those who question the prevailing narratives, dismissing them as fringe or irrational thinkers. However, genuine truth seekers remain undeterred by such judgments and maintain their steadfast commitment to uncovering the truth, regardless of the opinions of others.

The need marks the journey for intellectual rigor. Truth seekers analyse evidence meticulously, critically evaluate information, and engage in deep research to separate fact from fiction. They understand that truth can be elusive and requires a disciplined and rigorous approach to navigate the sea of information, biases, and conflicting viewpoints.

Amidst the challenges, the committed truth seeker stays resolute. They recognize that the pursuit of truth is a task that takes time to complete. It requires patience, resilience, and an unyielding spirit. They persist in their exploration, even when it seems like an uphill battle, understanding that the rewards of discovering and sharing the truth far outweigh the difficulties encountered along the way.

Ultimately, the truth-seeking journey is a noble and courageous endeavour. It is a pursuit driven by an innate curiosity, a thirst for knowledge, and a deep desire to understand the world in its most authentic form. Despite the resistance, skepticism, and hostility they encounter, truth seekers persevere, driven by the belief that the truth, once revealed, can bring about positive change, and create a more enlightened and just society.

Throughout history, individuals driven by an insatiable

thirst for truth have emerged as critical catalysts in driving meaningful transformations and questioning established narratives. These relentless truth seekers have wielded their intellectual and moral prowess to expose corruption, unravel concealed realities, and shape the course of public discourse. Their unwavering dedication has made invaluable contributions to society, fostering transparency and accountability and propelling progress across various domains.

Investigative journalists occupy a prominent place among these truth seekers. Fearlessly delving into the depths of complex issues, they have unearthed scandals, brought wrongdoing to light, and held the powerful accountable. By doggedly pursuing leads, conducting extensive research, and meticulously piecing together evidence, investigative journalists have shattered illusions and offered the public unfiltered access to the truth. Their work has often exposed systemic failures, challenged the status quo, and catalyzed legal and societal reforms.

Scientists, driven by the pursuit of knowledge and understanding, have also played a pivotal role as truth seekers. Through rigorous experimentation, meticulous observation, and unbiased analysis, they have unraveled the natural world's secrets. Scientists have challenged prevailing dogmas, debunked pseudoscience, and expanded our collective understanding of the universe. Their commitment to empirical evidence and intellectual integrity has helped society advance, fostering innovation, technological breakthroughs, and evidence-based decision-making.

Whistleblowers, courageous individuals who expose

hidden truths from within organizations, have made significant contributions as truth seekers. These brave individuals have risked their personal and professional well-being by exposing misconduct, fraud, and abuses of power. Whistleblowers have sparked public outrage, triggered investigations, and instigated essential reforms by shedding light on internal malfeasance. Their actions have helped prevent further harm, promote justice, and fortify the ethical foundations of various institutions.

Human rights activists, driven by a deep sense of justice and compassion, have tirelessly sought truth in the face of oppression, discrimination, and social injustice. Their tireless efforts to expose human rights abuses, advocate for marginalized communities, and challenge oppressive regimes have affected change. Human rights activists have amplified the voices of the oppressed, raised awareness of systemic injustices, and mobilized global support to bring about tangible improvements in human rights protections.

Collectively, truth seekers have reshaped societies, challenging complacency, and inspiring critical thinking. By providing accurate information, scrutinizing power structures, and speaking truth to power, they have fostered a more informed citizenry and nurtured democratic ideals. Their unwavering commitment to truth, justice, and progress has dismantled falsehoods, promoted transparency, and catalysed positive social change.

In an era marked by rapid dissemination of information and growing challenges to truth, the role of truth seekers remains as vital as ever. Their tireless pursuit of reality continues to be a beacon of hope, ensuring that no corruption, deception, or prevailing narrative goes unchallenged. As they champion transparency, accountability, and progress, truth seekers lay the foundation for a more equitable, just, and enlightened society.

While the term "truth seekers" is broad and encompasses a diverse range of individuals and approaches, their unwavering dedication to uncovering the truth and shedding light on obscured realities is the underlying thread that unites them. These truth seekers come from all walks of life, representing various fields of study, professions, and ideologies. They share a joint mission—challenging the status quo, questioning assumptions, and pursuing the unvarnished truth.

At the heart of their endeavor lies an insatiable curiosity and a relentless pursuit of knowledge. Truth seekers understand that ability is not static but a constantly evolving entity requiring exploration and discovery. They are driven by a deep desire to understand the world around them, to dig deeper than surface-level information, and to uncover hidden truths that may have been overlooked or deliberately obscured.

One of the defining characteristics of truth seekers is their willingness to ask difficult questions. They do not settle for easy answers or superficial explanations. Instead, they probe deeper, often venturing into uncomfortable territories to challenge prevailing narratives and uncover underlying realities. By doing so, they encourage critical thinking and foster intellectual discourse, promoting a more robust and well-informed society.

Evidence forms the cornerstone of a truth seeker's methodology. They recognize that mere assertions or beliefs are insufficient in discerning the truth. Instead, they seek solid evidence, rigorously examine facts and data, and apply sound reasoning to reach informed conclusions. This commitment to evidence-based inquiry helps separate fact from fiction, creating a more Reliable knowledge base for society at large.

In their quest for truth, these seekers often challenge conventional wisdom. They understand that established norms and widely accepted beliefs can sometimes hinder progress and prevent the exploration of alternative perspectives. By daring to challenge the status quo, truth seekers open new possibilities and pave the way for innovation and breakthroughs. Their willingness to embrace intellectual dissent inspires others to question deeply ingrained assumptions and explore uncharted intellectual territories.

Truth seekers understand that the pursuit of truth is not a solitary endeavour. They engage in constructive dialogue, collaborate, and build communities dedicated to seeking and disseminating knowledge. These communities foster an environment where ideas can be freely exchanged, and intellectual growth is nurtured. Truth seekers amplify their collective impact by coming together and creating a powerful force that drives positive societal change.

In a constantly evolving world, truth seekers serve as beacons of intellectual integrity and critical thinking. They remind us of the importance of questioning, investigating, and remaining open to new information. Their dedication to the pursuit of truth and the dissemination of knowledge elevates society, encouraging others to think critically, challenge assumptions, and strive for a deeper understanding of our complex world.

Ultimately, truth seekers embody the spirit of enlightenment, reminding us that the search for truth is a lifelong journey that requires intellectual curiosity, open-mindedness, and the willingness to confront uncomfortable truths. Their unwavering commitment to uncovering the truth is a powerful reminder that knowledge is a never-ending quest and that our collective understanding of the world can continuously be expanded and refined.

Chapter Three:
Religion and the Battle for Truth

R eligion, a guiding force for billions of people, has profoundly impacted human history, encompassing both a source of profound truths and a powerful instrument of deception. This chapter delves into the intricate dynamics that arise when religious realities clash with the manipulation and control of the masses through the manipulation of faith. Throughout the ages, from the tumultuous era of the Crusades to the fracturing divisions caused by religious schisms, and even in contemporary times with the prevalence of exploitative televangelism, we witness a complex interplay between genuine spiritual guidance and the cynical exploitation of faith for personal gain. Within this intricate tapestry of human experience, we explore the multifaceted dimensions of religion, contemplating its potential for enlightenment and salvation as well as the disheartening instances when it has been perverted to serve selfish interests[15].

Religious Great Dialogue for Truth

Once upon a time, a dreamland town called Aramthai existed in a world divided by beliefs and ideologies. It was a realm of immense diversity where people from various cultures and backgrounds coexisted harmoniously. In Aramthai, religion significantly influenced the lives of its inhabitants, shaping their values, traditions, and social structures.

The land of Aramthai was a mosaic knitted with threads of countless faiths, each belief system deeply rooted in the hearts and minds of its followers. The people of Aramthai held their convictions with unwavering dedication, embracing their unique religious practices as an integral part of their identities. Within the boundaries of Aramthai, sacred temples, churches, mosques, and synagogues stood side by side, representing the multifaceted spiritual tapestry of the land. People engaged in rituals, prayers, and ceremonies, seeking solace, guidance, and a connection to something greater than themselves. The vibrant hues of faith permeated every aspect of their existence, from how they dressed to how they interacted with one another. However, alongside the beauty of diversity, Aramthai had its challenges. The battle for truth was a constant undercurrent in the lives of its inhabitants. With beliefs so deeply ingrained, clashes between different religious factions occasionally erupted, fueling tension and ideological disputes.

Despite the conflicts, Aramthai became a crucible where the people, aware of their differences, also recognized the value of mutual respect and understanding. In this dream-land, interfaith dialogues blossomed, providing a platform for open conversations, shared experiences, and bridging gaps between belief systems. Wise sages, scholars, and spiritual leaders emerged, promoting harmony, and encouraging cooperation in pursuing collective truth.

Aramthai was a realm where individuals, regardless of their religious affiliations, found common ground in their shared humanity. They celebrated diversity as a source of strength, allowing the different belief systems to enrich their lives rather than divide them. Through empathy and compassion, they nurtured an environment where everyone's voice was heard and respected.

The quest for truth went beyond religious boundaries in this extraordinary land, Aramthai. It extended to pursuing knowledge, scientific exploration, and philosophical contemplation. Scholars and thinkers from all walks of life delved into the mysteries of the universe, embracing faith and reason as complementary facets of the human experience. The people of Aramthai believed that the more they understood the world around them, the more they could appreciate the magnificence of the divine.

As generations passed, Aramthai continued to evolve. The land became a beacon of tolerance, where acceptance and love transcended differences. The inhabitants of Aramthai thrived in their collective journey, ever inspired by the shared desire to unravel the mysteries of existence and to live in harmony, guided by the values of compassion, respect, and understanding.

And so, in the land of Aramthai, the people discovered that their diverse beliefs united them in the pursuit of truth and the celebration of their shared humanity. In this realm, the battle for truth was not a source of division but a catalyst for growth, enlightenment, and the eternal quest for a deeper understanding of the world they called home.

In the heart of Aramthai, nestled amidst breathtaking landscapes, trees canopies, and shimmering rivers, a majestic city named Amatjang stood. It was a place that epitomized unity and diversity, a testament to the power of harmony among people from different walks of life. Amatjang was renowned throughout the region for its grand temples, each dedicated to another faith, showcasing the city's commitment to honouring the multitude of religious beliefs embraced by its inhabitants.

As one wandered through the vibrant streets of Amatjang, a palpable sense of tranquility prevailed. The city exuded an aura of acceptance and tolerance, with followers of various religions cohabiting and respecting one another's deeply held beliefs. It was a remarkable mosaic where adherents of different faiths mingled freely, sharing their customs, traditions, and wisdom, creating a tapestry of spiritual diversity.

The grand temples of Amatjang were architectural marvels, rising proudly towards the heavens and adorning the skyline with their intricate designs and ethereal beauty. Each temple was a sanctuary of worship, a sacred space that echoed with prayers, hymns, and chants. The faithful flocked to these revered places, seeking solace, guidance, and a connection with the divine.

However, beneath the surface serenity of Amatjang, a subtle undercurrent simmered, hinting at a profound competition for dominance over truth among the religious communities. While the outward harmony prevailed, there existed an unspoken quest among the faithful to prove the righteousness and superiority of their respective faiths. It was a silent rivalry fueled by the human desire for affirmation and the belief that one's truth was the ultimate truth.

The religious leaders, custodians of their respective faiths, engaged in intellectual debates and discussions, striving to defend and promote their beliefs as the ultimate path to enlightenment. These debates, conducted with respect and civility, were often centred around interpretations of sacred texts, the nature of divinity, and the purpose of human exis-tence. The leaders sought not only to strengthen the faith of their followers but also to win the hearts and minds of those who remained undecided.

While these debates were typically carried out with intel-lectual rigor, occasionally, passions ran high, and tempers flared. During these moments, the competition for domi-nance over truth became more apparent as individuals became emotionally invested in defending their faith against perceived challenges or threats. However, the essence of Amatjang always prevailed, and disputes were eventually resolved through dialogue and compromise, reinforcing the city's commitment to peaceful coexistence.

This subtle competition for dominance over truth, although simmering beneath the surface, was not a detriment to the overall harmony of Amatjang. Instead, it acted as a catalyst for intellectual growth, encouraging individuals to explore the depths of their faith, question established beliefs, and seek a deeper understanding of the divine. It fueled a continuous quest for knowledge and wisdom as each religious community sought to refine and evolve its experience of truth.

The city of Amatjang, with its grand temples and harmonious balance, remained a beacon of religious diversity and acceptance. It stood as a testament to the human capacity to embrace differences, fostering an environment where the pursuit of truth was an ongoing journey celebrated by all. In Amatjang, the subtle competition for dominance over reality was not a source of division but rather a unifying force, as the people of the city recognized the beauty and value of engaging in a collective exploration of faith and spirituality.

Within Amatjang, a vibrant town nestled amidst rolling hills and blooming fields, a young man named Deng lived. His presence was fresh air, as his insatiable interest and open-mindedness shone through in every aspect of his life. From an early age, Deng's inquisitive nature led him down countless paths of discovery, constantly seeking to broaden his horizons and embrace the world's wonders.

Deng's upbringing played a significant role in shaping his character. He was fortunate to grow up in a household where religious tolerance was not only accepted but actively encouraged. His parents, Abuk, and Kuol were devout individuals who followed different faiths. Abuk is a Roman Catholic while Kuol is a Seventh Day Adventist follower. Despite their divergent religious beliefs, they managed to forge a harmonious union, recognizing the beauty and value in their differences. Together, they created a nurturing environment that celebrated diversity and emphasized the importance of seeking truth and understanding in a world filled with varied and often contrasting beliefs.

Deng was exposed to a rich arras of religious traditions and spiritual practices from an early age. He witnessed his mother participating in the rituals of her faith with grace and devotion while his father immersed himself in the teachings of his religious community. Instead of being confined by these differences, Deng's parents used their individual beliefs as steppingstones to foster discussions on shared values, morality, and the fundamental quest for enlightenment.

This atmosphere of religious acceptance cultivated within Deng a deep respect for all belief systems and a genuine desire to comprehend the essence of each. His youthful mind was like an unquenchable sponge, eager to soak up the knowledge and wisdom emanating from the diverse religious perspectives surrounding him. Deng developed an expansive worldview that transcended narrow boundaries through countless conversations, visits to places of worship, and engaging with individuals from various faiths.

Deng's open-mindedness and intellectual curiosity extended far beyond the realm of religion. He delved into the spaces of science, philosophy, art, and literature, seeking to understand the intricate interplay of these disciplines and their impact on human existence. His insatiable appetite for knowledge propelled him into a lifelong journey of exploration, where he eagerly sought to unravel the mysteries of the universe and his place within it.

In Amatjang, Deng became known not only for his thirst for knowledge but also for his unwavering empathy and respect for others. He became a beacon of harmony, bridging gaps between people of different faiths and backgrounds, fostering meaningful conversations, and encouraging dialogue that transcended superficial differences. In a world where prejudices often festered, Deng's genuine interest in understanding others helped break down barriers and fostered an environment of mutual respect and acceptance.

Deng's story serves as a reminder that it is possible to find unity amid diversity. Through his unwavering curiosity, open-mindedness, and the foundation of religious tolerance laid by his parents, Deng embraced a world filled with diverse beliefs, seeking to understand rather than judge. In doing so, he enriched his own life and became a catalyst for harmony and understanding within the community of Amatjang and beyond.

One day, as Deng leisurely strolled through the vibrant and bustling streets of Amatjang, a thriving city renowned for its diversity and cultural richness, he found himself captivated by an extraordinary sight. His eyes were drawn towards a gathering near the heart of the city, just a stone's throw away from the central square. Curiosity ignited within him as he noticed people from all walks of life converging, their faces alight with anticipation.

It was an occasion unlike any other—the Great Dialogue for Truth. The air crackled with electric energy as the leaders of Amatjang significant religions had come together, setting aside their differences, and embracing a shared commitment to open and honest discourse. The city, known for its harmonious coexistence among various religious beliefs, had seized the opportunity to celebrate its diversity while seeking a deeper understanding of one another.

The central square, usually abuzz with daily activities, had been transformed into a grand stage for intellectual exchange and respectful debate. A makeshift podium stood tall, its presence commanding attention. Around it, a sea of eager faces filled the air with a palpable sense of excitement and expectation. Deng couldn't help but be drawn closer, his footsteps quickening as he joined the multitude.

As he neared the central square, Deng found himself enveloped by a cacophony of voices, each one expressing a unique perspective, belief, and ideology. The crowd's diversity mirrored the rich tapestry of Amatjang itself, as people from all faiths, cultures, and backgrounds had gathered in unity, bound by a shared desire to explore the truths that guided their lives.

At the forefront of the gathering, the leaders of Amatjang major religions stood side by side, their expressions displaying a blend of solemnity, respect, and unwavering commitment to the pursuit of knowledge. Dressed in the distinctive garb of their respective faiths, they exuded an atmosphere of wisdom and humility, ready to engage in a series of thoughtful discussions that would challenge their beliefs and inspire profound introspection.

Deng's eyes darted between the participants, eagerly trying to grasp the essence of this monumental event. He marvelled at the diverse group before him—imams, rabbis, priests, monks, and spiritual leaders from various traditions, all gathered on this historic occasion. Each leader radiated a deep sense of reverence for their faith, yet they were united by a common goal—to forge bridges of understanding and build upon the foundations of mutual respect.

As the Great Dialogue for Truth commenced, the central square became a sanctuary of intellectual exchange. Passionate debates erupted, interlaced with moments of profound insight and profound empathy. The leaders took turns presenting their perspectives, drawing upon their sacred texts, philosophical teachings, and personal experiences to articulate their beliefs. Their words painted a rich tapestry of knowledge and contemplation, inviting the audience to witness the beauty and complexity of religious thought.

Enthralled by the weighty discussions unfolding before him, Deng found himself engrossed in a sea of profound ideas and heartfelt reflections. He listened intently, witnessing moments of genuine empathy and deep connection emerging amidst the debates. Through the power of words, the leaders aimed to bridge the gaps between their faiths, dispel misconceptions and foster an atmosphere of unity, despite their theological disparities.

Throughout the day, the Great Dialogue for Truth continued to captivate the hearts and minds of all present. It became a testament to the power of open dialogue as the leaders engaged in a heartfelt quest to understand one another, transcending their differences, and embracing the common threads that wove through their spiritual journeys.

By the time the sun descended on the horizon, a sense

of accomplishment and shared enlightenment saturated the atmosphere. The Great Dialogue for Truth had achieved its purpose—to foster understanding, mutual respect, and harmony among the diverse religious communities of Amatjang. As the crowd dispersed, leaving the central square imbued with a renewed sense of unity, Deng carried the profound experiences and lessons of the day within his heart, knowing that the seeds of understanding sown today would bear fruit in the days and years to come.

Deng left with the promise that he must attend the discussion the following day. Throughout the night, Deng's could not suppress the prospect of witnessing another truly significant day. As the night was quite long for Day, it eventually break and multitude of people started to gather in the town square again. As the debates commenced, Deng had already positioned himself in a spot that afforded him a clear view of the stage, ready to absorb the intellectual exchange that was about to unfold. The air was thick with anticipation, and a peaceful silence fell over the crowd as the religious leaders took their positions, preparing to present their arguments.

With bated breath, Deng listened intently to the orators as they stepped forward, each poised and eloquent, armed with an arsenal of persuasive rhetoric. The religious leaders passionately conveyed the comprehensive details of their respective belief systems, compellingly arguing why their doctrine represented the ultimate truth. Their words carry symbols of faith, blending logic and emotion to sway the minds and hearts of those in attendance.

Initially, the discussions were a genuine quest for

understanding, a platform for open dialogue and enlightenment. The arguments put forth by the religious leaders were thought-provoking, challenging Deng's preconceived notions and pushing the boundaries of his understanding. He marvelled at their knowledge depth, ability to quickly articulate complex ideas, and unwavering conviction.

However, as the debates progressed, a subtle shift began. What had started as a respectful exchange of ideas gradually transformed into a battle for supremacy. The religious leaders became increasingly entrenched in their positions, no longer seeking common ground or mutual understanding. Instead, a sense of rivalry and competition permeated the atmosphere, overshadowing the pursuit of genuine enlightenment. The once-civil discourse now gave way to veiled insults and subtle jabs. Rather than engaging in productive dialogue, the religious leaders resorted to rhetoric designed to belittle and undermine their opponents belief system. The noble quest for truth was eclipsed by the desire to assert dominance and emerge victorious.

Disheartened by this unexpected turn of events, Deng's initial enthusiasm waned. What had initially promised to be a transformative experience now felt tainted by the discord that had consumed the discussions. He yearned for a return to the spirit of genuine exploration and understanding, where different perspectives could coexist and thrive rather than engage in a futile battle for supremacy.

In the end, Deng's enthusiasm for witnessing history had been replaced by a bittersweet disappointment. As he left the gathering, he couldn't help but ponder the significance of this disheartening transformation. It served as a stark reminder of the fragility of intellectual discourse and the need for genuine empathy and humility in the pursuit of knowledge.

Amid the passionate debates swirling through the air, a hushed anticipation settled over the gathering. Amidst the enthusiasm, a figure emerged from the crowd, exuding an aura of wisdom and grace. Arek, a venerable elder, commanded immense respect from the people of Amatjang for her impartiality and profound understanding of diverse religions; as her presence commanded attention, a ripple of quiet reverence spread through the assembled multitude.

Arek weathered face bore the lines of countless experiences, and her eyes, shimmering with the light of wisdom, scanned the faces before her. With deliberate steps, she made her way to the centre, where a platform awaited her. The crowd's murmurs faded into silence, eagerly awaiting her words of wisdom. Sensing the moment's gravity, Arek raised her hand, signalling for stillness. The noise subsided, and a profound calm settled over the gathering. The weight of her presence resonated with the seekers of truth and the curious minds yearning for guidance.

Arek voice, rich with a timbre that commanded attention in the hallowed silence, resonated through the air. "My dear friends," she began, her words flowing like a soothing melody, "amid this passionate exchange, let us pause to reflect, breathe, and listen. Through silence, we can truly hear the echoes of our souls and find the path that unites us all."

Her words carried the weight of experience and the profound understanding she had gained through a lifetime of contemplation and study. Arek impartiality was well-known, as she had delved deep into the teachings and wisdom of various religions, forging a remarkable bridge between different faiths.

Arek voice continued, each word carefully chosen to impart both empathy and enlightenment. "In our quest for truth, let us remember that the essence of all religions is rooted in compassion, love, and understanding. They may diverge in their practices and beliefs, but at their core, they seek to guide us towards harmony and connection."

She gestured toward the diverse crowd, encompassing people of different backgrounds, beliefs, and ideologies. "We stand here, united by our shared humanity. Let us set aside our differences and embrace the vast collections of perspectives that binds our world together. Only through respectful dialogue and genuine curiosity can we unravel the complexities of existence and cultivate a deeper understanding of one another."

As her words resounded within the hearts of the audience, Arek presence seemed to transcend time and space, bridging the gap between past and future, tradition, and progress. Her call for unity and empathy resonated deeply with those gathered, igniting a collective longing for harmony and a shared vision of a brighter future.

With her final words, Arek voice swelled with hope and compassion. "Let us embrace this moment of silence not as a void but as a sacred opportunity to connect, to learn from one another, and to build bridges of understanding that will transcend the boundaries of our debates. Together, we can shape a world where compassion and respect guide our actions, knowledge, and understanding illuminate our path, and unity prevails over division."

Arek speech lingered in the air, leaving an indelible impression on the hearts and minds of those present. A wave broke the resounding silence of applause, a harmonious chorus of appreciation for her shared wisdom and guidance. Inspired by her words, the crowd rekindled their commitment to thoughtful discourse, seeking common ground while embracing the richness of their differences.

"Dear friends," she continued, "we have all come together on this auspicious occasion, united by a common purpose—to embark upon a journey of seeking truth, unburdened by the need to prove the superiority of any particular faith. Our gathering today is a testament to our shared commitment to fostering a genuine understanding that transcends the boundaries of belief systems and embraces the essence of humanity." Her carefully chosen words flowed gracefully through the air, captivating the hearts and minds of those in attendance. Each syllable carried the weight of her unwavering conviction and the sincerity of her intent. With each passing moment, her eloquence carries a sense of unity, urging everyone to embrace the profound interconnectedness that binds us all.

"In our quest for truth," she continued, her voice a gentle beckoning, "we must recognize that genuine understanding blossoms from the seeds of empathy, compassion, and an unwavering commitment to maintaining an open mind. Through empathy, we can truly grasp the experiences and perspectives of others to feel their joys and sorrows as if they were our own. Compassion enables us to extend a helping hand, alleviate suffering, and foster a world of kindness and harmony. And an open mind, unencumbered by preconceived notions or biases, allows us to embrace new ideas, to challenge our own beliefs, and to grow beyond the confines of our limited perspectives."

As her words settled in the hearts of those gathered, a profound silence permeated the room, enveloping the listeners in a shared contemplation. Everyone reflected upon the deep wisdom bestowed upon them, recognizing the transformative power of these principles in their own lives and the potential for collective enlightenment.

"With the fire of truth burning within us," she concluded, her voice now carrying a gentle enthusiasm, "let us pledge to honour the bonds that unite us, to engage in fruitful dialogue, and to embrace the diversity that enriches our journey. By fostering a world that celebrates empathy, compassion, and an open mind, we can forge a future where understanding prevails over ignorance, love triumphs over hatred, and unity conquers division."

Her words lingered in the air, leaving an indelible mark upon the hearts of those who had the privilege to witness this extraordinary moment. In that room, amidst the shared dedication to seeking truth, a collective resolve formed—a testament to the power of empathy, compassion, and an open mind in shaping a world where the quest for understanding would forever transcend the confines of faith and humanity would find its most authentic expression.

Arek proposal presented a fresh perspective, diverging from the prevalent path of division and conflict. She envisioned a transformative approach centred around unity and harmony. Rather than dwelling on their differences, she urged the religious leaders to embark on a collective service journey to their community.

Arek emphasized the need for these leaders to temporarily put aside their divergent beliefs and ideologies, encouraging them to join forces and work in unison. By actively collaborating to tackle the shared challenges experienced by the inhabitants of Amatjang, they would discover a common purpose that transcended their religious backgrounds.

The religious leaders would create a renewed sense of understanding and empathy through concerted efforts and shared endeavours. Their collaborative actions would act as bridges, linking their communities together and fostering connections previously hindered by discord.

Arek vision was rooted in the belief that through acts of service, the religious leaders would benefit the community and experience personal growth. By engaging in meaningful work side by side, they would witness firsthand the transformative power of unity and shared purpose, realizing that their shared humanity outweighed their religious disparities.

As these leaders stood together, addressing the needs of the people of Amatjang, they would inspire others to follow suit. Their collective efforts would ripple throughout the community, kindling a spirit of collaboration and understanding among its inhabitants. By embracing Arek proposition, they would sow the seeds of a harmonious future where respect and cooperation flourished, transcending religious boundaries and uniting people in their shared pursuit of a better tomorrow.

Initially skeptical of Arek proposal, the religious leaders found themselves in deep contemplation upon hearing her words. As her ideas permeated their thoughts, they began grasping the profound wisdom in her suggestion. They recognized that their ongoing ideological debates had hindered progress and divided their followers, ultimately limiting their ability to impact the world positively.

In this moment of reflection, the religious leaders acknowledged the urgent need to set aside their differences and redirect their energies towards a greater purpose: serving the common good. They understood that by relinquishing their dogmas and joining forces, they could transcend their limitations and unleash a collective passion for positive change.

With a renewed sense of unity, the religious leaders embarked on a journey of collaboration and cooperation. They convened gatherings where open dialogue replaced heated arguments, and mutual understanding returned to rigid adherence to doctrines. Through genuine conversations, they discovered shared values transcending religious boundaries, realizing their goal was to foster peace, compassion, and justice.

Their collective efforts began reverberating beyond religious communities, inspiring people from various backgrounds to join the cause. Their actions spoke louder than words, serving as a testament to the transformative power of unity and collaboration. By placing the greater good above their individual beliefs, the religious leaders demonstrated that spiritual teachings could be a unifying force, guiding humanity toward a brighter and more harmonious future.

In time, the ripple effect of their joint endeavours spread far and wide, reaching individuals, communities, and nations. Their example challenged long-held stereotypes and preconceptions, fostering interfaith dialogue, and nurturing a culture of respect, empathy, and cooperation. The once-skeptical religious leaders became beacons of inspiration, igniting a global movement that transcended religious boundaries and redefined the role of faith in a rapidly changing world.

Ultimately, Arek proposal proved to be a catalyst for profound transformation. It united religious leaders who had once been divided by ideological differences and inspired them to redirect their energies toward serving the greater good. Through their collective efforts, they created a legacy of unity, compassion, and positive change that resonated across generations, leaving an indelible mark on history.

Driven by a deep sense of compassion and a shared commitment to improving the lives of others, the religious communities of Amatjang embarked on a series of collaborative initiatives. Recognizing the power of education to uplift individuals and communities, they established schools that provided quality education to children from all backgrounds. These institutions became beacons of knowledge, fostering an inclusive learning environment where students were nurtured and empowered to realize their full potential.

Healthcare, another critical area of focus, was addressed by establishing hospitals and medical facilities. Staffed by

dedicated professionals from different faiths, these institutions provided essential medical services to individuals
regardless of their religious affiliations. Here, the sick and
vulnerable received compassionate care, and lives were
saved through innovative treatments and advanced medical
technologies.

In addition to formal institutions, the religious communities of Amatjang recognized the importance of reaching out
directly to those in need. They launched outreach programs
that extended their support to marginalized populations, irre-
spective of their religious beliefs. These programs aim to
alleviate poverty, provide necessities, and empower individuals to overcome adversity. Whether through food drives,
vocational training, or counselling services, the communities
worked hand in hand to uplift the underprivileged and foster
a sense of hope and dignity.

As the religious communities collaborated, they discovered a profound revelation: the shared values underpinning
their respective beliefs were remarkably similar. Love,
compassion, and the collective desire to create a more just
and harmonious world became the guiding principles that
bound them together. They realized that despite their different religious doctrines and rituals, at the core, their faiths
converged on the fundamental principles of kindness, empathy, and the pursuit of social justice.

Through their collaborative efforts, the religious communities of Amatjang not only made tangible improvements in
the lives of individuals and the community and set a powerful example for others to follow. Their unity and dedication

shattered stereotypes and fostered greater interfaith understanding and respect. Amatjang became a beacon of hope
and a testament to the transformative power of religious
communities working together for the betterment of society.

In the wake of their achievements, the people of Amatjang
experienced a profound shift in their collective consciousness. The community became more inclusive, embracing
diversity and celebrating the richness that different faith traditions brought to their lives. The walls that had once divided
them crumbled, giving way to a shared vision of unity and
cooperation.

Under Arek wise and compassionate guidance, the religious communities of Amatjang stood as a shining example
of what could be achieved when people set aside their differences and come together to address common challenges.
Their legacy endured, inspiring future generations to harness
the strength of their diversity and collaborate towards creating a world where love, compassion, and the pursuit of a
better future prevailed.

Over time, as the days turned into years, the people of
Amatjang bore witness to a remarkable transformation—the
transformative power of unity. What was once a city plagued
by divisions and conflicts gradually emerged as a shining
beacon of religious tolerance, where the battle for truth transcended its intellectual confines and evolved into a collective
pursuit of harmony and understanding.

The journey towards this profound change was challenging. Amatjang had long been a melting pot of diverse religious
beliefs, each with genuine followers and passionate leaders.

These differences had fueled animosity and competition in the past, resulting in a fractured community. However, as the need for unity grew more apparent, a profound shift began to take place within the hearts and minds of the people.

Recognizing the destructive nature of their past disputes, the citizens of Amatjang sought a new path that emphasized collaboration and respect. They realized that true strength lay not in division but in collective action and cooperation. This realization paved the way for the city's remarkable transformation.

Once entrenched in their rivalries, religious leaders played a pivotal role in this paradigm shift. As they witnessed the changing tide and recognized the potential for a brighter future, they set aside their differences and embarked on a journey of reconciliation. These once bitter competitors found common ground and forged unexpected friendships, their shared vision of a harmonious Amatjang fueling their resolve.

The religious leaders became allies, not only in theory but also in practice. They led their respective followers by example, demonstrating the power of understanding and acceptance. They held interfaith dialogues, fostering an environment where open conversations could occur without fear of judgment. Together, they organized events that celebrated the diversity of religious traditions, fostering a spirit of inclusivity and mutual respect.

As the leaders set aside their egos and focused on the greater good, their followers followed suit. The people of Amatjang witnessed firsthand the positive impact of unity and embraced the values of tolerance and compassion. Walls that had once separated them began to crumble, replaced by bridges of understanding that spanned the city.

The transformation was not instantaneous, but it was relentless. With each passing year, Amatjang blossomed into a haven of religious tolerance, attracting attention and admiration from neighbouring communities and beyond. People from far and wide flocked to Amatjang, inspired by the city's remarkable journey and eager to learn from its example.

Amatjang became a place where diversity was tolerated and celebrated in this newfound unity. It became a haven for individuals of various faiths, each finding solace and acceptance within its borders. The city's strength lay in its ability to weave together the tapestry of different beliefs, recognizing that the pursuit of truth was not a solitary endeavour but a collective effort.

The transformative power of unity had breathed new life into Amatjang, forever altering its trajectory. It stood as a testament to the potential for change, reminding the world that the human spirit could transcend differences and create a better future even in the face of deep-seated divisions. Through their collective pursuit of harmony and understanding, the people of Amatjang had transformed their city into an enduring symbol of religious tolerance, a beacon of hope for generations to come.

Moved by wisdom and leadership of Arek, the community of Amatjang added a prestigious suffix, 'dit' to her name, which means 'The Great or venerable' in English. Her name change from Arek to Arekdit (Arek the Great). The religious leaders follow suit by pooling their resources and built a hospital in her name; 'THE AREKDIT HOSPITAL'.

Deng, deeply moved by the extraordinary transformation he had witnessed, made a profound decision to devote his entire life to the noble cause of promoting unity and fostering tolerance among people from all walks of life. Inspired by the transformative journey of Amatjang, he embarked on a remarkable quest, traveling to distant lands and diverse communities, carrying with him the powerful message of unity and acceptance.

Deng's journey took him across continents, where he encountered individuals from various cultures, backgrounds, and beliefs. With each encounter, he shared the inspiring story of Amatjang, illustrating the incredible potential for personal growth, understanding, and harmony that can arise when people embrace diversity and bridge their differences.

Through his passionate storytelling, Deng captivated audiences with vivid accounts of Amatjang journey, highlighting his challenges, his lessons, and his ultimate transformation. Deng emphasized the importance of empathy, compassion, and open-mindedness in creating a world where everyone is valued and respected.

Deng encouraged dialogue in every land he visited and facilitated meaningful conversations between individuals who had previously been estranged due to their differences. He organized workshops, conferences, and interactive events, creating safe spaces for people to share their stories, exchange perspectives, and build bridges of understanding. Deng aimed to dismantle the barriers that often divide societies and promote a sense of global kinship by fostering mutual respect and fostering a sense of shared humanity.

As Deng's tireless efforts and the profound impact of his message spread, communities worldwide began to embrace the ideals of unity and tolerance. Through his dedication and unwavering commitment, Deng inspired countless individuals to question their preconceived notions, challenge their biases, and strive for a more inclusive and harmonious world.

Deng's journey continued unabated as he tirelessly traversed the globe, spreading his message of unity and tolerance to even the Earth's most remote corners. His work became a beacon of hope, igniting a global movement that transcended borders, cultures, and ideologies. From bustling cities to isolated villages, people were awakened to the power of embracing diversity and celebrating the richness it brings to our shared human experience.

Ultimately, Deng's unwavering determination and the ripple effect of his efforts brought about a tangible change. Communities that were once torn apart by fear and prejudice began to heal, fostering environments of acceptance and cooperation. Through his storytelling and unwavering commitment, Deng left an indelible mark on the world, inspiring generations to embrace unity, empathy, and tolerance as the foundations for a brighter and more harmonious future.

Chapter Four:
Media and the Post-Truth Era

With the advent of mass media, a revolutionary era emerged, giving birth to an entirely new dimension in the age-old struggle between truth and deception. This chapter explores the rise of propaganda, misinformation, and the infamous phenomenon known as "fake news." Here, we shall traverse the elaborate web of how media, once a tool for information dissemination, transformed into a potent weapon to manipulate public opinion, ignite political agendas, and fabricate alternate realities that have sometimes shaken the foundation of objective truth.

The dawn of mass media marked a pivotal shift in human history, granting unprecedented access to information and communication across vast distances and diverse populations. However, this newfound power came with inherent risks, as the potential for distortion and manipulation of information grew exponentially.

Propaganda, which has a long history dating back centuries, found renewed vigor in the era of mass media. Governments, organizations, and individuals recognized the immense influence wielded by the media and exploited it to advance their objectives. By disseminating biased or misleading information through various media channels, they sought to sway public opinion, shape perceptions, and maintain or gain control over the masses.

Misinformation, which is either intentionally spread or inadvertently shared due to negligence, further complicated matters. In a world where information travels at the speed of light, false or misleading content could spread like wildfire, muddying the waters of truth, and blurring the lines between fact and fiction. This phenomenon led to a crisis of trust as people struggled to discern reliable sources from deceitful ones.

The advent of social media platforms brought a paradigm shift in the way information was consumed and disseminated. These platforms initially envisioned as connecting individuals and fostering open dialogue, inadvertently became breeding grounds for the proliferation of misinformation and "fake news." The algorithms behind these platforms, designed to maximize user engagement, often prioritized sensational and polarizing content, incentivizing the rapid spread of unverified or biased information.

With the barrier between truth and falsehood becoming increasingly porous, the notion of objective truth itself was challenged. In this environment, alternate realities emerged, constructed by various interest groups to suit their narratives and agendas. The public lived in echo chambers, surrounded by information that reinforced their beliefs, while contradictory facts were easily dismissed or labelled as "fake."

This chapter will delve into the mechanisms by which misinformation and propaganda are disseminated, the psychology behind their effectiveness, and their profound consequences on society and democratic processes. Moreover, we will explore the efforts made to combat this modern-day challenge, including fact-checking initiatives, media literacy programs, and the role of responsible journalism in preserving the integrity of information.

In conclusion, the rise of propaganda, misinformation, and "fake news" in the age of mass media has posed unprecedented challenges to our perception of truth and reality. To address this complex issue, it is crucial to understand the mechanisms at play, promote critical thinking skills, and foster a media ecosystem that prioritizes accuracy, transparency, and the pursuit of genuine understanding. We can only navigate the vast sea of information and arrive at a more informed and enlightened society.

The term "post-truth era" signifies a distinct and concerning period in human history, characterized by a significant shift in how public opinion is shaped and influenced. Unlike when objective facts and evidence played a central role in determining beliefs and perspectives, the post-truth era is marked by a profound change in how information is received and processed[16].

During the late 2010s, this concept gained widespread attention and recognition, primarily due to its prevalence in the political and media landscapes. In an era where emotions and personal beliefs have taken precedence over factual accuracy, the foundation of public discourse and decision-making has been substantially altered.

One of the critical challenges in the post-truth era is the proliferation of misinformation, disinformation, and the spread of so-called "fake news." Often disseminated through social media and online platforms, these falsehoods can potentially deceive and manipulate people's perceptions[17]. In this environment, the credibility of traditional media outlets, which have historically been relied upon to provide accurate information, has been called into question.

As a result of these changes, the way people consume and interpret information has undergone a radical transformation. Individuals are increasingly drawn to sources that confirm their preexisting beliefs and opinions, creating echo chambers and reinforcing existing biases. Critical thinking and fact-checking, once essential for discerning truth from falsehood, have become less common, as emotional appeal and sensationalism tend to sway public sentiment more effectively.

The post-truth era has had profound implications for democracy and public discourse. In political contexts, it has allowed populist leaders and movements to gain traction by appealing to emotions and identity, often at the expense of rigorous policy discussions based on evidence. The diminished influence of objective facts also creates fertile ground for spreading conspiracy theories, further contributing to societal polarization and mistrust.

Addressing the challenges posed by the post-truth era requires a multifaceted approach. Promoting media literacy and critical thinking skills is crucial to empowering individuals to navigate the vast sea of information and discern truth from fiction. Fact-checking initiatives and responsible journalism are pivotal in holding information disseminators accountable and restoring trust in credible sources.

Furthermore, technology companies and social media platforms are responsible for combating the spread of misinformation and disinformation on their platforms by implementing robust content moderation and verification processes.

In conclusion, the post-truth era represents a turning point in how information is disseminated, received, and perceived. The diminished influence of objective facts and the rise of emotional appeals and personal beliefs have profound implications for public opinion, democracy, and societal cohesion. Navigating this era necessitates collective efforts to promote critical thinking, fact-checking, and responsible information dissemination to foster a more informed and resilient society.

Several factors have contributed to the rise of the post-truth era:

1. Social Media

The democratization of information sharing through social media platforms has revolutionized how people communicate, interact, and consume content. These platforms have become powerful tools that enable individuals from all walks of life to share their thoughts, opinions, and creative expressions with a global audience. As a result, we have witnessed unprecedented connectivity and engagement among people worldwide.

However, this newfound freedom in content publishing comes with its drawbacks. Compared to traditional media outlets with stringent fact-checking and editorial oversight, social media platforms often need comprehensive mechanisms to verify the accuracy and reliability of the content shared. This deficiency has led to the propagation of false information and misleading narratives, commonly known as "fake news."

The rapid spread of false information on social media can have far-reaching consequences. Misleading narratives can polarize communities, influence public opinions, and affect political landscapes. Additionally, the viral nature of social media allows misinformation to reach vast audiences in hours or even minutes, making it challenging to effectively contain and correct false claims.

Moreover, social media algorithms play a significant role in shaping the content users see. These algorithms are designed to prioritize content that elicits engagement and reactions, amplifying sensational or provocative information. As a result, factually incorrect or misleading content can gain disproportionate visibility and traction, further exacerbating the spread of misinformation.

To address this challenge, various stakeholders, including social media companies, governments, and civil society, have been grappling with finding practical solutions. Social media platforms have taken steps to combat misinformation by partnering with fact-checking organizations, flagging disputed content, and limiting the reach of misleading posts. However, the balance between curbing misinformation and preserving free speech remains contentious and complex.

Additionally, media literacy education has become crucial in empowering individuals to evaluate the content they encounter on social media critically. By teaching people how to recognize misinformation, understand biases, and fact-check information, society can equip individuals with the tools to navigate the digital landscape more responsibly.

In conclusion, while the widespread use of social media has democratized information sharing and empowered countless individuals, it has also opened the floodgates to the rapid spread of false information and misleading narratives. Finding the right balance between freedom of expression and the prevention of misinformation is a pressing challenge that requires collaborative efforts from various stakeholders to foster a more informed and responsible digital society.

2. Filter Bubbles and Echo Chambers

Filter bubbles and echo chambers are two prominent phenomena in the modern digital age, brought about by how social media platforms curate and deliver content to their users. These algorithms are designed to learn from users' behavior, interests, and preferences, to enhance user engagement and keep them on the platform for longer. However, the unintended consequence of these algorithms is the formation of insular information environments that limit exposure to diverse viewpoints and perspectives.

2.1 Filter Bubbles

A filter bubble is a phenomenon that characterizes the personalized information landscape users find themselves in within the realm of social media platforms. This phenomenon arises from the intricate workings of algorithms that meticulously curate content to align with a user's historical interactions, clicks, likes, and shares. As users progressively engage more with specific genres of content, these algorithms progressively constrict the array of information they are exposed to. Consequently, users become immersed in a digital environment saturated with content that validates and fortifies their existing beliefs, affinities, and predispositions.

To illustrate, consider an individual who consistently consumes articles revolving around environmental concerns and actively advocates for sustainable practices. In such a scenario, the algorithm governing their content feed is inclined to prioritize the presentation of content related to environmentalism. Simultaneously, it might downplay or even exclude content that could potentially present contrary viewpoints or alternative perspectives on the topic.

This phenomenon encapsulates the notion that online platforms, driven by intricate algorithms, can inadvertently

confine users within echo chambers of their own preferences. While the aim is to enhance user engagement and
satisfaction by delivering content that resonates with their
interests, this personalized curation can unintentionally
create a homogeneous digital sphere that shields users from
diverse viewpoints. Consequently, filter bubbles can contribute to reinforcing pre-existing beliefs, impeding exposure to
contrasting ideas, and ultimately limiting the potential for
constructive dialogue and a well-rounded understanding of
complex subjects.

In essence, filter bubbles exemplify the delicate interplay
between user preferences and algorithmic content curation,
underscoring the need for conscious efforts to seek out
diverse perspectives and engage with a broad spectrum of
information, both online and offline.

2.2 Echo Chambers

An echo chamber is a digital manifestation of the human
tendency to seek out and associate with like-minded individuals, creating a virtual space where opinions reverberate
and amplify without encountering the friction of opposing
viewpoints. This phenomenon is an evolution of the filter
bubble concept, in which algorithms and personal preferences
conspire to present individuals with content that aligns with
their existing beliefs, preferences, and interests.

In this virtual enclave, like-minded individuals find
solace and camaraderie among others who share similar

perspectives. It's within these insular online communities that individuals encounter an environment that reinforces their convictions, often serving to shield them from dissenting opinions. Within these echo chambers, interactions are laden with affirmation and validation, providing a sense of belonging and camaraderie that can be appealing in a rapidly changing and complex world.

The dynamics within echo chambers can lead to a self-perpetuating cycle. As individuals interact with others who echo their views, their beliefs gain strength and conviction through repetition and validation. The absence of dissenting voices and contrary information further cements their ideas, as the natural process of critical analysis is stifled.

However, the allure of echo chambers comes at a cost. The exchange of ideas becomes stagnant, and the ability to engage in meaningful discourse with individuals who hold differing opinions diminishes. This confinement to a singular perspective can be detrimental to a well-rounded understanding of complex issues and can hinder personal growth through exposure to new ideas.

One of the most concerning aspects of echo chambers is the nurturing of confirmation bias. This cognitive bias prompts individuals to seek out and pay attention to information that aligns with their preexisting beliefs, while disregarding or dismissing opposing viewpoints. The echo chamber environment acts as a fertile ground for this bias to flourish, as users are consistently fed information that only reinforces what they already believe. This reinforcement can occur even if the information being consumed is based on misinformation or inaccurate data, perpetuating false notions and misconceptions.

The consequences of echo chambers ripple beyond the digital realm. They can contribute to polarization in society, making it increasingly difficult for people with differing perspectives to engage in constructive dialogue. This can hinder the democratic process, as compromise and understanding are essential for effective governance and decision-making. Recognizing and addressing the existence of echo chambers is crucial for promoting open discourse, critical thinking, and the pursuit of truth in an increasingly interconnected world.

3. Polarization and Divisiveness

In an era characterized by the rapid dissemination of information and the proliferation of online communication platforms, the phenomenon of polarization and divisiveness has emerged as a significant concern. Central to this issue are the concepts of filter bubbles and echo chambers, which play pivotal roles in shaping societal discourse and interactions. Filter bubbles, fueled by algorithms and personalized content delivery, create virtual environments where individuals are predominantly exposed to information and viewpoints that align with their preexisting beliefs and preferences. As people are served content tailored to their interests, they are inadvertently shielded from perspectives that challenge or differ from their own. This isolation within echo chambers results in a narrowing of intellectual horizons, fostering a sense of affirmation that can be both comforting and confining.

Echo chambers, on the other hand, amplify this effect by creating self-reinforcing feedback loops. When individuals interact primarily with like-minded individuals, their opinions are echoed back to them, reinforcing their initial convictions. This reinforcement leads to a heightened sense of tribalism, where individuals perceive those within their ideological circles as allies and those outside as adversaries. The consequences of these dynamics are far-reaching. As society becomes increasingly compartmentalized into distinct ideological groups, the avenues for constructive dialogue and the exploration of common ground become constricted. The once-rich landscape of civil discourse, where individuals from different walks of life engaged in meaningful conversations, is replaced by a fragmented landscape of disconnected islands of thought.

Moreover, the lack of exposure to diverse viewpoints fosters an environment where mistrust and animosity can flourish. When individuals are shielded from alternative perspectives, it becomes easier to caricature those with differing opinions, leading to a dehumanization of the "other." This dehumanization, in turn, paves the way for the growth of distrust, prejudice, and even hatred. The challenge lies in finding ways to bridge these gaps and counteract the divisive forces at play. Fostering media literacy and critical thinking skills can empower individuals to navigate the complex landscape of information more effectively. Encouraging open dialogue, both online and offline, can create spaces where individuals from different backgrounds can come together to exchange ideas and perspectives.

In essence, the issue of polarization and divisiveness is a multifaceted one that demands a concerted effort from individuals, communities, and technological platforms alike. By acknowledging the dangers of filter bubbles and echo chambers, and actively seeking out diverse viewpoints, society can begin the process of restoring a more inclusive and empathetic discourse that embraces the richness of human perspectives.

4. Challenges for Objective News and Quality Journalism

In the modern media landscape, the pursuit of objective news reporting and quality journalism faces a multitude of challenges, and one of the most significant adversaries comes in the form of social media algorithms. These algorithms, designed to cater to user preferences and maximize engagement, inadvertently contribute to the erosion of reliable and balanced news coverage. The implications of this trend are far-reaching, impacting not only the way information is disseminated but also the broader societal understanding of critical issues.

Social media platforms, with their vast user bases and intricate data-driven systems, have become primary sources of news consumption for a significant portion of the population. However, these platforms operate on algorithms that are built to amplify sensational and emotionally charged content. This preference for the dramatic and eye-catching has profound consequences for the state of objective news reporting.

Rather than valuing well-researched, nuanced, and balanced reporting, these algorithms tend to prioritize clickbait articles and sensational headlines that are likely to elicit strong emotional reactions from users. As a result, news stories that play on outrage, fear, or excitement often receive higher visibility and engagement, overshadowing more thoughtful and rigorous pieces of journalism. This not only skews the overall news landscape but also shapes public perception by reinforcing stereotypes, stoking polarization, and focusing attention on surface-level issues rather than underlying complexities.

This shift towards emotionally charged content poses a fundamental challenge to the principles of objective journalism. Objective reporting seeks to present information in a fair and impartial manner, allowing readers to form their own conclusions based on well-researched facts. However, the algorithm-driven emphasis on sensationalism can lead to the distortion of information and the prioritization of shock value over accuracy. This undermines the credibility of news sources, eroding the trust that is essential for a functioning democracy and an informed citizenry.

Furthermore, the reliance on clickbait and sensationalism has real-world consequences for the economic sustainability of quality journalism. As platforms incentivize content that garners high engagement, news organizations might feel pressured to produce more sensationalized stories to maintain relevance and financial viability. This can divert resources away from investigative journalism and in-depth reporting, which require time, resources, and expertise. Consequently, the public is left with a dearth of well-researched and context-rich content that is necessary for understanding complex societal issues.

Addressing these challenges requires a multi-pronged approach. Media literacy education becomes crucial in helping individuals distinguish between reliable, objective reporting and sensationalized content. News organizations should prioritize their commitment to rigorous reporting and consider alternative revenue models to reduce their reliance on algorithm-driven platforms. Additionally, social media platforms can play a role by tweaking their algorithms to reward accuracy, balance, and depth, rather than just engagement metrics.

In conclusion, the sway of social media algorithms towards sensational and emotionally charged content presents a formidable obstacle to the pursuit of objective news reporting and quality journalism. Navigating this challenge requires collective efforts from news organizations, platforms, policymakers, and the public to ensure that credible and balanced information continues to be a cornerstone of informed societies.

5. Diminished Critical Thinking

In an era where information flows abundantly and effortlessly, a concerning trend has emerged – the erosion of critical thinking skills. As individuals immerse themselves in digital environments tailored to their preexisting beliefs, the very foundation of their ability to assess information objectively starts to erode. This phenomenon, known as filter bubbles and echo chambers, presents a formidable challenge to the pursuit of truth and rational discourse.

The human mind, in its quest for cognitive ease, finds comfort in consuming content that resonates with its established viewpoints. However, this very comfort can become a double-edged sword. The constant exposure to agreeable narratives creates a cognitive shortcut that diminishes the motivation to question the validity of the information encountered. In this landscape, critical thinking takes a backseat as individuals become passive recipients rather than active evaluators of information.

This lack of critical engagement has alarming consequences. Misinformation and disinformation find fertile ground in these echo chambers, gaining unwarranted credibility and spreading like wildfire. The unchecked sharing of misleading content perpetuates falsehoods, deepens societal divisions, and weakens the collective foundation of knowledge.

Tackling the intricate issue of filter bubbles and echo chambers necessitates a multi-pronged strategy that involves a collective effort from all stakeholders. Social media platforms, as influential gatekeepers of information, must embrace their role responsibly. Diversifying content presentation by deliberately exposing users to a broader spectrum of perspectives can puncture the echo chamber's walls. Algorithms designed to prioritize engagement over accuracy need recalibration to prioritize information quality and diversity.

Yet, the onus doesn't solely fall on platforms. Empowering individuals with media literacy skills becomes paramount. Educating users to recognize the markers of bias, misinformation, and logical fallacies arms them with the tools to navigate the digital landscape critically. Equipped with this knowledge, users can break free from the confines of their personalized information bubbles and seek out diverse viewpoints.

However, the solution transcends digital realms and seeps into society at large. Encouraging open, respectful dialogues among individuals with contrasting opinions fosters a culture of intellectual growth. Engaging in constructive conversations demands active listening, empathy, and a willingness to consider alternative viewpoints. Such exchanges challenge preconceived notions, nudging individuals towards a more comprehensive understanding of complex issues.

Ultimately, the path to dismantling filter bubbles and echo chambers demands a conscious commitment to intellectual curiosity. Actively seeking out dissenting opinions, engaging in rigorous fact-checking, and cultivating an environment where ideas can clash without hostility can lead to a transformational shift. By breaking down the barriers that confine us to comfortable silos of thought, we can pave the way for a society that thrives on well-rounded perspectives, informed decision-making, and a shared sense of empathy and unity.

6. Distrust in Traditional Media

In recent years, a significant shift in the public's perception of traditional media outlets has emerged, with many individuals expressing skepticism and disillusionment. This phenomenon, known as "distrust in traditional media," has become increasingly prevalent and has profoundly influenced how people consume information and engage with the news[20].

The origins of this widespread distrust can be traced back to various factors. One prominent issue lies in the perception of bias that some individuals attribute to mainstream media organizations. Critics argue that these outlets often favor specific ideologies or agendas, leading to a lack of objectivity and impartiality in their reporting. This perceived bias, whether real or perceived, has eroded the credibility of traditional media in the eyes of many, fueling their desire to explore alternative sources of information.

With the rise of the digital age and the proliferation of social media, the avenues for accessing news and information have multiplied manifold. While this has granted people unprecedented access to diverse perspectives and viewpoints, it has also resulted in an influx of unvetted and Unreliable sources. In their quest for untainted information, people have turned to non-traditional platforms, some of which may need more rigorous fact-checking processes or adhere to professional journalistic standards.

Although often questionable in credibility, these alternative sources of information resonate with segments of the population that feel marginalized or overlooked by main-stream media. This has created echo chambers, where like-minded individuals reinforce their existing beliefs and opinions, further deepening societal polarization.

Additionally, the rapid dissemination of information through digital channels has amplified misinformation and disinformation. False narratives, conspiracy theories, and deliberately misleading content can now reach millions in hours, sowing confusion and eroding public trust in all forms of media.

The consequences of this distrust of traditional media are far-reaching. In a democratic society, an informed citizenry is essential for effective decision-making and holding those in power accountable. When trust in reputable news sources diminishes, the potential for manipulation and the proliferation of false narratives increases, undermining the foundations of a healthy democracy.

To address this complex issue, media organizations must strive to regain public trust by prioritizing transparency, accuracy, and inclusivity in their reporting. Emphasizing the value of fact-checking, ethical journalism, and unbiased reporting can help restore credibility and foster a more informed, engaged, and united society.

Furthermore, media literacy programs are crucial in equipping the public with the skills to evaluate information sources and discern Reliable reporting from misinformation critically. By empowering individuals to navigate the vast sea of information with discernment, they can make more informed decisions and actively participate in constructive public discourse.

In conclusion, distrust in traditional media is a multifaceted and consequential development that has reshaped information consumption in the modern world. As the media landscape continues to evolve, efforts to rebuild trust, promote media literacy, and uphold journalistic integrity are indispensable for safeguarding the democratic principles that underpin society. Only through collective responsibility and a commitment to truth can we navigate the complexities of the digital age and foster a more informed and harmonious global community.

7. Political Polarization

In highly polarized societies, people tend to be more receptive to information that supports their political ideologies, regardless of its factual accuracy. This exacerbates the spread of misinformation and reinforces divisions in society. Political polarization is a phenomenon that significantly influences communities, shaping the way people consume and process information. In highly polarized societies, individuals become more susceptible to favoring and accepting information that aligns with their existing political beliefs and ideologies, even if such details lack factual accuracy or evidence. This cognitive bias, known as confirmation bias, can profoundly affect public discourse, the media landscape, and the overall dynamics of society[21].

When people are exposed to information that resonates with their preexisting beliefs, they embrace it unquestioningly. This behavior creates an echo chamber effect, where like-minded individuals reinforce each other's viewpoints and dismiss contradictory information. Consequently, the exchange of diverse perspectives becomes increasingly limited, hindering open dialogue and rational debate, essential for a healthy democracy.

The consequences of this echo chamber effect are far-reaching. Firstly, it fosters the rapid spread of misinformation and disinformation. False narratives, half-truths, and even outright lies can gain momentum within ideologically aligned groups, quickly spreading across social media platforms and other communication channels. As a result, people become misinformed and misguided, further solidifying society's existing divisions.

Secondly, political polarization can amplify the emotional intensity of political discussions. When people feel that their core beliefs are under attack, they may become defensive and unwilling to consider alternative viewpoints. This emotionally charged atmosphere can lead to hostility and hatred, eroding the civility necessary for constructive political dialogue.

Moreover, polarization can hinder cooperation and compromise between political factions and parties. As ideological rigidity increases, the chances of finding common ground diminish, making it more challenging to address critical societal issues effectively. In such an environment, policymakers may prioritize political gains over the greater good, contributing to governmental gridlock and inefficiency.

Furthermore, the media landscape in polarized societies can become highly segmented, with each faction seeking sources that reinforce its worldview. This leads to media bubbles, where individuals are exposed to a narrow range of opinions, further entrenching their preexisting beliefs, and limiting exposure to diverse perspectives.

Overcoming political polarization requires a concerted effort from various stakeholders, including political leaders, media organizations, educational institutions, and individual citizens. Encouraging media literacy and critical thinking skills can help individuals become more discerning information consumers. Promoting open dialogue, respectful discourse, and fact-based discussions can foster a more inclusive and tolerant society.

Political leaders should prioritize policies that bridge divisions and seek common ground rather than perpetuating partisan divides. Moreover, nurturing a sense of national identity transcending political affiliations can help unite societies around shared values and goals.

In conclusion, political polarization presents significant challenges to societies worldwide. By recognizing the impact of confirmation bias and echo chambers and actively promoting understanding and cooperation, communities can address this issue and foster a more informed, tolerant, and cohesive future.

8. Disinformation Campaigns

State and non-state actors have increasingly used social media platforms to spread disinformation and sow discord in foreign countries. These efforts aim to undermine trust in institutions and destabilize democratic processes. Disinformation campaigns have become a significant global concern, with state and non-state actors leveraging the power of social media platforms to propagate false information and foster chaos within foreign countries[22]. Digital communication channels have provided these actors unprecedented opportunities to disseminate misleading narratives and manipulate public opinion.

At the core of these campaigns lies a deliberate intent to erode trust in established institutions and create an atmosphere of uncertainty, thus weakening the foundations of democratic processes. These actors aim to sow seeds of doubt, polarize societies, and disrupt the cohesion necessary for effective governance by targeting vulnerable population segments and exploiting existing divisions.

In this era of instant communication and the interconnectedness of social media, disinformation can spread like wildfire, reaching millions of individuals within moments. The speed and scale of dissemination make it challenging for truth and fact-checking to catch up, allowing false information to persist and cause significant harm.

State actors like foreign governments may resort to disinformation campaigns to achieve various geopolitical objectives. They might seek to undermine a rival nation's credibility, delegitimize their institutions, or influence the outcome of important political events, such as elections or referendums. By exploiting the openness of social media platforms, these state actors can obfuscate their involvement and amplify divisive content through fake accounts, bots, and automated networks.

Non-state actors, including extremist groups and ideological organizations, have also actively disseminated disinformation. They use these campaigns to advance their agendas, recruit followers, and provoke societal unrest. Sometimes, these groups may exploit genuine grievances to foster discontent and drive susceptible individuals toward violence or radicalization.

The consequences of such disinformation campaigns can be severe. They can lead to a breakdown in social cohesion, increase political polarization, and amplify existing social tensions. Moreover, the erosion of trust in institutions undermines the very foundation of democratic governance, weakening the collective ability to address complex societal challenges effectively.

Efforts to combat disinformation are ongoing, but the task remains formidable. Technology companies, governments, civil society organizations, and individual users are all part of the broader effort to identify and limit the spread of false information. Fact-checking initiatives, algorithmic adjustments, and increased user awareness are some measures being taken to address this pressing issue.

Addressing disinformation requires a multifaceted approach combining technological advancements, policy frameworks, and critical media literacy education. By fostering a society that values and demands accurate information, we can fortify our democracies against the corrosive effects of disinformation and ensure a more informed and resilient citizenry.

The role of traditional media in the post-truth era is

complex. While some traditional media outlets adhere to rigorous fact-checking and journalism ethics, others may prioritize sensationalism and biased reporting to cater to specific audiences or increase viewership. This dichotomy further blurs the lines between credible journalism and biased reporting, leading to a loss of trust in the media.

Combating the challenges posed by the post-truth era requires a multifaceted approach. It involves promoting media literacy to help individuals critically evaluate information, improving fact-checking and verification processes, holding social media platforms accountable for curbing misinformation, and encouraging media outlets to prioritize accurate and unbiased reporting.

Addressing the post-truth era requires the collective efforts of governments, technology companies, media organizations, and individuals to ensure that objective facts and evidence-based reporting remain integral to public discourse and decision-making.

Chapter Five:
Deception in Politics and Governance

Politics and deception have been inextricably linked throughout human history. This captivating chapter delves deep into the records of political intrigue, manipulation, and the unscrupulous exploitation of power. Drawing on a vast historical canvas, we embark on a riveting journey that unravels the evolution of cunning stratagems from the days of Machiavelli to the contemporary realm of modern political campaigns. Brace yourself as we navigate the turbulent waters where leaders have skillfully wielded deception as a potent weapon to solidify their dominance and manipulate the masses.

At the heart of this exploration lies the enigmatic figure of Niccolò Machiavelli, a renowned political philosopher, and strategist from the Renaissance era. His seminal work, "The Prince," introduced a groundbreaking governance perspective involving a pragmatic approach to wielding power. Machiavelli's unapologetic endorsement of deception as a legitimate means to achieve political objectives left an indelible mark on subsequent political leaders.

Throughout history, Machiavellian principles have been subtly or overtly incorporated into the practices of those in power[23]. Intrigue and manipulation became critical tools in the arsenal of rulers, aiming not only to secure their positions but also to expand their dominion. From medieval courts with their labyrinthine plots to the cutthroat world of Renaissance politics, the seeds of deception were sown into the very fabric of governance.

Similarly, in the ancient kingdom of Wu, a young and cunning prodigy named Sun Tzu rose to prominence as a skilled deceiver. With an insatiable thirst for knowledge and a sharp intellect, he gained the trust of the king, becoming one of his most valued advisors. As news of an impending invasion by the powerful kingdom of Wei reached their ears, Sun Tzu saw an opportunity to wield the power of deception. Manipulating the council with skillful lies and half-truths, Sun Tzu convinced them to adopt his deceitful strategies for the impending battle. He emphasized the importance of gathering intelligence on the enemy's weaknesses while obscuring his true intentions and motivations. While some questioned his methods, Sun Tzu's charisma and persuasiveness won them over, and they eagerly embraced his web of deception.

When the day of the battle arrived, the Wu forces appeared unprepared and vulnerable, allowing the Wei army to underestimate them. However, it was all part of Sun Tzu's grand deception. As the battle ensued, he cunningly manipulated the enemy's perceptions, leading them into traps and using their assumptions against them. His psychological warfare disoriented and demoralized the Wei forces, causing confusion and chaos. While the council and generals were initially bewildered by Sun Tzu's actions, they soon realized the brilliance of his deception as the Wu forces gained the upper hand. By the time the dust settled, the enemy was defeated, and the kingdom of Wu emerged victorious.

Sun Tzu's mastery of deception became legendary, and his book, "The Art of Deception," chronicled his ingenious methods, securing his place in history as a master of deceit. His legacy served as a cautionary tale, reminding generations to come to that deception, when wielded with intelligence and precision, could be a potent weapon in the hands of a cunning strategist.

As societies progressed and democratized, the methods of political deception evolved as well. The advent of mass communication, especially in the form of newspapers, radio, television, and eventually the internet, presented political figures with an unprecedented platform to sway public opinion. Propaganda emerged as a powerful tool, skillfully used by leaders to create carefully crafted narratives that served their interests while diverting attention from inconvenient truths.

With their vast machinery and sophisticated marketing techniques, modern political campaigns further honed the art of deception. Spin doctors and strategists adeptly molded the public perception of candidates and issues, carefully crafting messages that appealed to specific demographics. In an age of information overload, distinguishing fact from fiction has become increasingly challenging for the average citizen.

However, the relationship between politics and deception is not solely characterized by malicious intent. Diplomacy, a fundamental aspect of international relations, often involves strategic ambiguity and veiled intentions. Skillful diplomats know how to balance truth and concealment to advance their nation's interests without causing unnecessary conflict.

Yet, the darker side of deception in politics remains ever-present. Scandals, cover-ups, and the deliberate manipulation of information have periodically shaken public trust in political institutions. In this chapter, we confront the unsettling reality that some leaders have prioritized their gains over the welfare of the populace they were meant to serve.

We must remain vigilant and discerning as we navigate this intricate web of deceit. Understanding the historical roots of political deception empowers us to be more critical consumers of information and less susceptible to manipulation. By shining a light on the shadows that lurk within the corridors of power, we equip ourselves with the knowledge needed to demand greater transparency and accountability from those who govern.

In conclusion, this chapter offers a thought-provoking exploration of the symbiotic relationship between politics and deception. From Machiavelli's and Sun Tzu cunning strategies to the ever-evolving landscape of modern political campaigns, we examine how deception has been employed as a potent instrument to achieve and maintain dominance. As we look to the future, armed with the wisdom of the past, we aspire to build a political landscape that upholds integrity, transparency, and the genuine empowerment of the people.

Cunning Advisors: The Tale of Gotnhom

Once upon a time, in the prosperous and peaceful land of Gotnhom, where rolling hills embraced lush valleys and crystal-clear rivers flowed gently through the countryside, there existed a majestic kingdom known far and wide for its fair and just governance. The harmonious coexistence of its diverse yet unified people was a testament to the wise leadership that guided them.

The heartwarming tales of contentment and prosperity reached far beyond the borders of Gotnhom, and travelers from distant lands spoke with admiration about the virtuous and transparent rulers who sat upon the throne. The kingdom's monarchs, who had reigned for generations, were beloved by their subjects, admired for their compassion, and revered for their dedication to the welfare of the realm.

However, amidst the glimmering facade of benevolence and the grandeur of the royal court, a shadowy truth lurked in the depths of the kingdom's politics and governance. Behind closed doors, within the opulent walls of the royal palace, a web of deception was being spun by those closest to power.

Unbeknownst to the trusting citizens of Gotnhom, a circle of ambitious and cunning advisers had woven a web of secrets, manipulation, and intrigue. These individuals, driven by their thirst for influence and control, aimed to shape the kingdom according to their desires, disregarding the well-being of the people they were meant to serve.

In the council chambers, where decisions that would impact the lives of countless citizens were made, whispered alliances and hidden agendas were the order of the day. The illusion of a utopian society was carefully maintained, skillfully crafted through carefully orchestrated public events and well-timed proclamations. Behind it all, the true intentions of these cunning advisers remained hidden in the shadows, unknown to the blissful populace.

As time passed, the noble rulers, unknowing of the machinations beneath the surface, continued to lead their kingdom with the utmost dedication and integrity, never suspecting the deceit that threatened to erode the very foundation of their cherished realm.

However, the fate of Gotnhom lay in the balance as the web of deception grew ever more vital. The once-transparent governance was now a maze of intrigue, with every step masked in uncertainty. Though still content in their day-to-day lives, the citizens were slowly affected by the insidious workings of a corrupted system.

Gradually, cracks appeared in the idyllic facade as some astute individuals started to unravel the truth. As whispers of treachery and deceit spread through the kingdom, a few brave souls sought to expose the sinister plot threatening their beloved land. Prominent members of the kingdom become vocal one after the other.

The tale of Gotnhom, once a story of blissful prosperity, was now a gripping narrative of hidden ambitions, power struggles, and the courage of those who dared to challenge the status quo. The kingdom's future hung precariously in the balance, and only time would tell whether the light of truth and justice could pierce through the darkness that had engulfed the realm of politics and governance.

At the heart of this deception lay King Awandit, a masterful and intelligent leader with an almost mesmerizing charisma and a sinister proficiency in manipulation. With honeyed words and a disarming smile, he effortlessly portrayed himself as the ultimate champion of the people, convincingly advocating for their rights and promising to bring about an era of prosperity and well-being.

King Awandit's public speeches were like enchanting symphonies that stirred the hearts of the masses, captivating them with lofty promises and grand visions. His silver-tongued orations resonated deeply with the people, forging an unwavering loyalty toward him. Citizens from all walks of life embraced him as the saviour they had longed for, a beacon of hope in an otherwise turbulent world.

Little did the unsuspecting populace know that a web of deceit and greed lurked behind the facade of benevolence. A veil of lies and half-truths obscured King Awandit's true intentions. Beneath his charming exterior, he harbored a lust for power and wealth that knew no bounds. The people's trust was not a means to an end but merely a steppingstone in his quest for total dominance.

Under the guise of progress, King Awandit enacted policies

that served only his self-interest and that of his inner circle. While he promised to improve the lives of his subjects, he cunningly manipulated the very systems he claimed to champion, ensuring that wealth and influence were concentrated in the hands of the elite few, including himself.

Those who dared to question or oppose him were swiftly silenced, for he possessed an intricate network of spies and enforcers who guarded his secrets and carried out his will without hesitation. Dissenters faced persecution and reprisals, making it clear that opposition to the King's rule was not tolerated. Many people have disappeared under unclear circumstances and their whereabout is still unknown.

As the years passed, King Awandit's reign revealed its dark underbelly. The people slowly began to grasp the cruel reality that they had been deceived, realizing that the promises of prosperity were hollow echoes in the face of their worsening conditions. Poverty, inequality, and corruption flourished under his iron fist, masked by an illusion of progress.

But even in the face of mounting evidence, the King's charisma remained an impenetrable shield, blinding many to the truth. His charisma acted as a potent elixir that seemingly absolved him of any wrongdoing in the eyes of his devoted followers.

Ultimately, the rise of King Awandit was a cautionary tale, a stark reminder that charisma alone does not define a true leader. Beneath the captivating surface, unchecked manipulation can breed tyranny and subjugation, leaving a nation trapped in the clutches of a false saviour who exploits their trust for personal gain. It serves as a solemn reminder that vigilance and critical thinking are vital in the face of persuasive rhetoric and that the true character of leaders must be scrutinized beyond the glittering façade they present to the public.

King Awandit, a cunning and intelligent ruler, skillfully established a formidable inner circle composed of nothing less than the most loyal and ambitious advisors the kingdom had ever seen. Awandit handpicked these trusted confidants, their hearts beating with his insatiable hunger for power and influence. He plans to die on the throne. With an unwavering loyalty to their King, the advisors swore an oath of secrecy and vowed to protect their tightly knit brotherhood at all costs. United by a shared vision of dominion and an unquenchable thirst for control, they formed an impenetrable fortress of intellect and cunning.

Within the hallowed walls of the royal council chambers, this select group of advisors, whose minds were as sharp as the finest blades, devised elaborate schemes with the utmost precision. Their strategies were as complex as the finest tapestries, intricately woven to preserve their grip on the kingdom and safeguard their true intentions from the prying eyes of the unsuspecting citizens.

Using their collective brilliance, they carefully orchestrated a grand facade, displaying an image of unity and benevolence to the world outside the palace walls. The citizens, blissfully unaware of the machinations happening in the shadows, lauded King Awandit, and his advisors as virtuous protectors of the realm. Behind closed doors, however, the truth revealed itself. The council of loyalists convened in clandestine gatherings, plotting, and scheming to further their web of influence. Each decision was calculated to maintain its stranglehold on power, ensuring that dissenting voices were silenced or eliminated without hesitation.

King Awandit's advisors mastered the art of manipulation, skillfully weaving a tapestry of lies to justify their actions and rationalize the sacrifices made for the greater good of the kingdom. Their true intentions were masked under layers of deception, leaving the kingdom's inhabitants utterly oblivious to the dangerous dance between light and shadow that governed their lives.

As time passed, the circle of loyal advisors grew bolder and more audacious in their pursuits. Their unyielding grip on power tightened, and dissent was met with swift retribution. The kingdom, seemingly tranquil on the surface, was a cauldron of secrets, intrigue, and betrayal boiling beneath.

The legacy of King Awandit and his advisors became one of both admiration and fear. While the kingdom flourished under their reign, those who dared to look beyond the dazzling facade glimpsed the darker truth lurking in the shadows.

In the annals of history, the tale of King Awandit and his inner circle would be forever etched, a story of ambition, power, and the lengths one would go to secure their place in the annals of control – a cautionary reminder that even the brightest of smiles can hide the darkest of intentions.

The courtiers employed a cunning array of devious tactics, chief among them being the insidious manipulation of information. At the heart of their Machiavellian scheme lay a meticulously crafted system designed to control and dictate news flow, ensuring that only narratives aligned with their regime's interests saw the light of day. This web of influence extended far and wide, ensnaring various communication channels and wielding them as potent tools of deception.

With their iron grip on information dissemination, the courtiers skillfully suppressed dissenting voices that dared to challenge their authority or question their actions. Through coercion, intimidation, and subtle threats, they instilled fear in those who might have otherwise spoken out against the injustices perpetrated by the ruling regime. As a result, the populace was left mainly oblivious to the truth, trapped in an illusionary world constructed by these master manipulators.

The courtiers, well-versed in psychological warfare, were masters at spreading disinformation and misleading narratives. False stories, skillfully crafted to divert attention from their misdeeds, were sown like seeds throughout the kingdom. These tales of distraction shifted blame, created scapegoats, and obfuscated the true nature of their actions, perpetuating an atmosphere of confusion and doubt among the people.

The courtiers controlled the press through a web of influential connections, manipulating journalists and writers to act as mere mouthpieces for their propaganda. The once-independent press now danced to the courtiers' tune, churning out articles and reports that glorified the regime's achievements and omitted any mention of its wrongdoings. This orchestrated charade played upon the vulnerability of human perception, leading many to embrace the distorted reality presented to them unwittingly.

Despite the tight stranglehold on information, some brave souls resisted, seeking to expose the truth and bring transparency to the kingdom. These dissenting voices, however, were systematically marginalized, their reputations tarnished, and their credibility questioned. The courtiers spared no effort in discrediting these truth-seekers, labeling them as troublemakers, heretics, or even traitors, aiming to isolate them from society and undermine their influence.

In the shadowy corners of the kingdom, whispers of the courtiers' dark tactics began to circulate clandestinely. Secret meetings, underground pamphlets, and encrypted messages became how the suppressed truth tried to resurface. These brave few risked their lives to keep the flame of dissent alive, daring to challenge the oppressive narrative and expose the courtiers' nefarious deeds.

However, the struggle for truth was not in vain. As the manipulative schemes of the courtiers grew more intricate, so did the resistance against their tyranny. The people's thirst for the truth, though suppressed, remained unquenchable. Slowly but surely, the cracks in the courtiers' grand façade began to appear, and the collective will of the populace ignited a fire of change.

Ultimately, history would remember the courtiers as skilled architects of deception and manipulating information as a dark stain on the annals of time. Yet, the memory of those who dared to challenge the status quo, who fought valiantly against the lies and deception, would be enshrined as symbols of hope and courage, paving the way for a future where truth and justice prevailed.

The cunning King and his wise advisors engaged in a web of clandestine affairs with neighboring kingdoms in their relentless pursuit to solidify and expand their dominion. Secluded in the shadows, they carefully orchestrated covert dealings to forge alliances that served their insatiable hunger for power and prosperity. However, the price of these hidden agreements was seldom borne by the privileged few at the top; instead, it was a burden heaved upon the unsuspecting shoulders of Gotnhom innocent citizens.

These concealed arrangements were intricately woven together, rooted in the premise of mutual interests. The King and his advisors spared no expense when it came to bending the course of diplomacy to their will, disregarding the welfare and well-being of their people in the process. Due to their insidious schemes, Gotnhom's citizens often suffered the consequences without knowing the true motivations behind their rulers' actions.

These secret alliances became a well-guarded arsenal in the monarch's quest for personal gain and their reign's preservation. Behind the opulent curtains of the court, riches flowed into the coffers of the elite, and the King's influence swelled like a colossal tide. As the common folk toiled and struggled in the shadows, they were kept blissfully ignorant of the sacrifices they were unwittingly making to sustain the King's supremacy.

In a paradoxical twist, the more the King and his advisors consolidated their power through these furtive dealings, the more disconnected they became from the plight of their subjects. The rulers' hearts grew colder, numbed by their ambition, as they reveled in the splendor of their ill-gotten wealth and impervious positions. The people's suffering was rendered invisible, shrouded in a veil of ignorance woven by the hands that should have protected and nurtured them.

Yet, even within the darkest corners of this shadowy intrigue, a flicker of hope remained. In the hearts of a few brave souls who dared to question the status quo, seeds of resistance were sown. As the truth slowly trickled out from beneath the veneer of deceit, a murmur of dissent echoed through the streets of Alek. Whispers of rebellion and discontent grew more robust with each oppressive decree, and a spark of resistance ignited the hearts of those who yearned for justice and transparency.

In the end, the tale of the King and his advisors' clandestine dealings serves as a stark reminder of the potential consequences when power is wielded without empathy and when the pursuit of self-interest overrides the collective welfare of a nation. The destiny of Gotnhom now hangs precariously in the balance as the people stand at the precipice, torn between remaining ignorant of their rulers' deception or daring to rise and reclaim their rights as rightful custodians of their fate.

As the relentless march of time pressed on, a subtle yet perceptible undercurrent of unease swept through the kingdom. Like a soft murmur, whispers of discontent began to echo in the streets and marketplaces, drifting from one person to another like a haunting melody. The once unwavering trust in their leaders now wavered, replaced by a growing sense of skepticism and doubt.

As the people observed the actions of those in power, they

couldn't help but question the motives behind their decisions and policies. Hints of hidden agendas and obscured intentions danced in their minds, leaving them with a gnawing feeling that something was amiss in their home realm.

Once regarded as a benevolent and just ruler, King Awandit seemed to have veiled his true self behind a carefully constructed facade. His courtiers, skilled in manipulation and flattery, played their parts flawlessly, adding layers of deception to the intricate web they wove around the throne.

Unraveling this tangled web of lies and half-truths became arduous for those who sought the truth. Each thread of deceit seemed to lead to another, creating a labyrinth that defied easy comprehension. As if obscured by a fog of confusion, the real intentions of the King and his court remained just beyond the reach of those who dared to question them.

In this climate of uncertainty, alliances were formed among the people - secret meetings in dimly lit taverns and hushed conversations in hidden corners. They exchanged tales of suspicion and shared fragments of information they had gathered, trying to piece together the puzzle that now defined their reality.

Yet, even as discontent grew, fear remained a powerful deterrent. The consequences of openly challenging the authority of the King and his court were dire, and dissenters knew all too well the price paid by those who dared to stand against the current. Thus, the populace was caught in a paradoxical dance, torn between their desire for truth and justice and the real threat that loomed over them.

Despite the daunting obstacles, a growing band of brave

souls journeyed to uncover the truth behind the veiled curtains of power. Each revelation they unearthed brought them closer to the deception's heart, illuminating the manipulative plot's intricacies.

As time passed, the kingdom stood at a precipice, and the whispers of discontent evolved into a relentless call for transparency and accountability. The realm's fate hinged on the delicate balance between the enigmatic facade woven by the King and the unwavering determination of those who sought the truth.

Little did they know that their actions, like ripples in a vast pond, would eventually culminate in a reckoning that would reshape the very foundations of the kingdom. For the deceptive web spun so meticulously by King Awandit and his courtiers could not remain impregnable forever, and the truth, no matter how obscured, had a way of revealing itself when the time was right.

Fortunately, not all hope was lost. In the darkest hours, a beacon of light emerged from the shadows, illuminating the path to truth and justice. This group of courageous and relentless individuals, aptly named the Truth-seekers, rose to the challenge with unwavering resolve.

As the deceptions and lies propagated by the powerful cast a suffocating blanket over Gotnhom, the Truth-seekers began their quest. They came from diverse backgrounds, bringing their unique skills and perspectives to the cause. United by a shared determination to uncover the hidden truths, they embarked on a perilous journey to expose the web of deceit that had ensnared their beloved land.

The Truth-seekers were led by charismatic figures who inspired countless others to join the noble mission. Among them was the brilliant and resourceful Amou, a former investigative journalist with an unyielding dedication to truth and justice. Alongside her was Lual, a tech prodigy whose hacking and digital forensics prowess proved invaluable in uncovering the layers of deception woven by the corrupt.

With the strength of their collective conviction, the Truth-seekers began meticulously gathering evidence and testimonials, revealing the sinister machinations of those who sought to maintain their grip on power. In their pursuit of truth, they faced numerous challenges, encountered dangerous obstacles, and encountered relentless opposition from the forces they sought to expose.

Yet, the Truth-seekers persevered, undeterred by the looming threats and risks. They established secret communication networks to ensure their findings reached sympathetic ears, all while eluding the watchful eyes of the deceivers. As the movement grew, more and more people rallied behind them, feeling compelled to reclaim their land from the clutches of dishonesty.

The Truth-seekers' campaign reached every corner of Gotnhom, empowering the people to question the status quo and demand transparency from their leaders. Their message resonated deeply, igniting a spark of hope in those who had felt powerless for far too long.

In the face of adversity, the Truth-seekers remained resolute, fueled by the knowledge that their sacrifices paved the way for a brighter future. With every revelation they brought to light, the deceptive foundation of the corrupt leaders crumbled, leaving them exposed and vulnerable to the demands of justice.

Finally, after many battles fought in the shadows and the public eye, the day of reckoning arrived. The Truth-seekers presented their irrefutable evidence, compelling even the most ardent defenders of deception to question their allegiance. The people's collective will could no longer be ignored as the truth spread like wildfire.

In a tidal wave of unity and determination, the citizens of Gotnhom rose, demanding justice and accountability. The oppressive grip of the deceivers weakened as the truth became a rallying cry, shaking the very foundations of their power. The courage and resilience of the Truth-seekers had ignited a revolution for transparency, and the wheels of justice began to turn.

Ultimately, the Truth-seekers triumphed, and Alek witnessed a transformation like never before. Transparency became the new norm, and accountability was instilled at every level of governance. The courageous actions of these individuals restored justice and rekindled the hope of a brighter, more honest future for their land.

The legacy of the Truth-seekers would live on, inspiring generations to stand against deceit and fight for truth, justice, and the greater good. Once shrouded in darkness, Alek was now a beacon of hope for those who yearned for a world guided by transparency, fairness, and the unwavering pursuit of truth.

Led by a young and fearless activist named Amel, the Truth-seekers, a determined and courageous group of like-minded individuals, embarked on a challenging and transformative journey that would forever alter the course of their kingdom's history. Fueled by an unyielding thirst for justice and unwavering courage, they set out to expose the clandestine machinations of the ruling elite, whose deceptive practices had trapped the kingdom in a web of lies and manipulation.

With her charismatic leadership and unshakable resolve, Amel rallied the Truth-seekers, a diverse cadre of passionate individuals, each possessing unique skills and strengths. Their hearts were aflame with a burning desire to unveil the truth and break the chains of deception that bound their people; they ventured into uncharted territories where few dared to tread.

Their journey took them to the darkest corners of the kingdom, where hidden documents lay concealed, and secrets whispered only in hushed tones. With each step, they encountered new challenges that tested their physical endurance and mental fortitude. Yet, they pressed forward, bolstered by their shared conviction and the belief that revealing the truth was paramount, regardless of the personal risks involved.

Together, they delved into the depths of corruption, unearthing a trove of incriminating evidence that exposed the truth about the ruling elite's evil actions. The pursuit of justice led them through intricate labyrinths of deceit, where they uncovered the extent of the manipulation inflicted upon the kingdom's people. Amidst the shadows and dangers surrounding them, they remained steadfast, never losing sight of their noble purpose.

Conducting secret interviews with whistleblowers and informants, the Truth-seekers pieced together the puzzle of deception bit by bit. Each revelation sent shockwaves through the kingdom, awakening a slumbering populace to the harsh reality they had been blind to for so long.

As their journey progressed, the Truth-seekers faced numerous trials, facing adversaries' intent on preserving the status quo. The ruling elite, terrified of their secrets being unveiled, attempted to quash the Truth-seekers' efforts with deceit, intimidation, and even outright violence. But, undeterred, Amel and her allies stood their ground, their unyielding dedication to the truth propelling them forward.

With the dissemination of their findings, the kingdom's people were roused from their complacency, uniting under the banner of truth and demanding accountability from their leaders. The once unchallenged power of the ruling elite began to crumble under the weight of public outrage, and a new era of transparency and justice was born.

Amel and the Truth-seekers' daring quest became the stuff of legends, inspiring generations to come. Their journey exemplified the transformative power of truth, courage, and unity in the face of deception and oppression. As the kingdom embarked on a path of reform and healing, they stood as a shining beacon, reminding all that even the most insidious deceptions could be dismantled by those willing to confront the truth head-on.

Amel and her companions embarked on a treacherous journey, fraught with countless challenges that tested their resilience and courage. From the outset, their path was

littered with insurmountable obstacles that seemed determined to impede their progress. Despite the dangers that lay
ahead, they remained resolute in their commitment to the
cause, knowing that the fate of Gotnhom depended on their
unwavering dedication.

In their pursuit of truth and justice, Amel and her allies
found themselves entangled in a web of espionage. Spies
lurked in the shadows, cunning and elusive, determined to
sabotage their every move. But the group's determination
was unyielding, and they skillfully navigated the dangerous
waters of espionage, gradually uncovering vital clues that
exposed the evil forces working against them.

Threats loomed large at every turn, forcing them to remain
vigilant. The enemies of progress were relentless in their
pursuit, attempting to intimidate and dishearten Amel and her
companions. Yet, they stood firm, undeterred by the shadows
of fear that sought to engulf them. Instead, these trials fueled
their resolve, making them even more steadfast in bringing
the truth to light.

As if spies and threats weren't enough, Amel and her allies
faced something far more sinister – attempts on their lives.
The forces of corruption were desperate to maintain their
stranglehold on Gotnhom's politics and governance, resort-
ing to violent means to silence those who dared to challenge
them. But Amel and her companions proved to be formidable
adversaries, skillfully evading danger and turning the tables
on those who sought to end their quest.

With each step forward, the group's perseverance bore
fruit. Revelations came to light, and the veil of deception

shrouded Gotnhom's political landscape began to lift. Their investigation unearthed a web of corruption that ran deep, tainting the foundations of the nation they loved. The tendrils of deceit extended far and wide, infecting even the highest echelons of power.

Despite the disheartening truths they uncovered, Amel and her companions refused to succumb to despair. Instead, they channeled their anger into a determination to fight for justice and cleanse Gotnhom of the corruption that had festered for far too long. Their shared purpose and unbreakable bond forged in the crucible of adversity became the driving force behind their quest.

As they worked together, united by a common cause, Amel and her companions inspired hope among the people of Alek. They became a beacon of light in the darkness, a symbol of resilience against overwhelming odds. Their bravery and commitment sparked a movement, rallying citizens from all walks of life to demand change and hold those responsible for corruption accountable.

Ultimately, Amel and her companions achieved more than they had envisioned. They exposed the sinister machinations of corruption within Gotnhom's politics and instigated a profound transformation in the nation's governance. Their journey had been a testament to the power of unwavering dedication and the indomitable spirit of those who dare to stand up against injustice. Through their sacrifices and unrelenting pursuit of truth, they left an enduring legacy that would forever shape Gotnhom's history.

As the news of the truth-seekers groundbreaking

discoveries reached every corner of Gotnhom, it swiftly transcended boundaries, spreading like wildfire among the populace. The revelations struck a chord with the people, igniting a fierce spark of resistance that had long smoldered beneath the surface. The once docile citizens, now awakened to their rulers' deceit, found within themselves the determination to challenge the oppressive regime that had held them captive for so long.

The streets of Gotnhom became a battleground of ideologies as well-informed and impassioned citizens united in their shared demand for accountability and change. The authoritarian rulers were taken aback by the sudden and unprecedented wave of dissent that surged through the kingdom, catching them off guard and leaving them scrambling to maintain control.

Mass protests erupted in every town and village, giving voice to the collective anger and frustration that had been suppressed for generations. The people's unyielding resolve was met with fierce resistance from the ruling elite, who sought to quell the uprising by any means necessary. But the citizens of Gotnhom were no longer cowed by fear; they had gained a new weapon in the form of knowledge, and their unity made them a force to be reckoned with.

The truth-seekers, who had risked everything to uncover the hidden truths, became symbols of hope and inspiration for the oppressed masses. They stood firm in the face of adversity, bolstered by the knowledge that their sacrifices paved the way for a brighter and more just future.

As days turned into weeks, the kingdom remained

embroiled in the turmoil of change. The oppressive regime attempted to suppress the protests with violence and propaganda, but the people's determination could not be extinguished. Instead, the brutal actions of the rulers served to fuel the flames of revolution even further.

In a surprising turn of events, some ruling elite members began to question their allegiance to the oppressive regime. Confronted with the undeniable evidence of their leaders' deceit, a few courageous individuals switched sides, joining the resistance ranks and supporting the demands for accountability.

International support also poured in as the news of the uprising spread beyond the kingdom's borders. Nations and organizations sympathetic to the plight of the Gotnhom people lent their voices to the chorus of calls for justice and reform—diplomatic pressure mounted on the oppressive regime, isolating them further globally.

The streets became a canvas of creativity and unity, with art, music, and solidarity becoming potent symbols of resistance. Peaceful demonstrations were held, conveying the strength of the people's resolve and their unwavering commitment to a better future.

As the movement grew in strength and numbers, the oppressive rulers found themselves cornered, with nowhere to escape the tides of change. The demands for accountability became impossible to ignore, and cracks began to form within the power structure.

Eventually, after months of relentless pressure and with the weight of their lies too burdensome to bear, the once-unshakable rulers finally crumbled. Faced with the undeniable truth and the unyielding will of the people, they were forced to step down from power, clearing the way for a new era of governance and transparency.

With the oppressive regime toppled, the citizens of Gotnhom stepped into a new chapter of their history. Guided by the truths uncovered by the brave truth-seekers, they began rebuilding their society with justice, fairness, and compassion at its core.

Though the journey was not without challenges, the united spirit of the people prevailed. The discoveries of the truth-seekers and the subsequent uprising changed the course of Gotnhom's destiny forever. It stood as a testament to the power of knowledge and the unbreakable spirit of a people united in their pursuit of truth, freedom, and a brighter tomorrow.

The pressure of mounting public outrage became an insurmountable force that King Awandit and his council could no longer ignore. Their once impregnable walls of denial and indifference began to crumble as discontent surged. It was an undeniable truth that their actions had ignited the fury of the masses, and they could no longer escape the consequences of their decisions.

Despite their initial attempts to quell dissent and maintain an appearance of authority, the voices of the people grew louder and more unified. Protesters filled the streets, demanding justice, and accountability. The King's advisors, who had once shielded him from the repercussions of his actions, now realized the gravity of their complicity in perpetuating injustice. The weight of guilt pressed upon them, urging them to rethink their loyalty to the throne.

Within the palace walls, the King and his council were faced with a critical juncture – a pivotal moment in which they had to decide between holding onto power at any cost or acknowledging their people's grievances. As they huddled in closed-door meetings, the echoes of dissent from the streets reverberated, seeping through the opulent chambers and casting doubt upon their previous certainties.

Eventually, the undeniable truth could no longer be ignored or concealed. The King and his advisors could no longer suppress the rising tide of public anger and were left with no choice but to confront the consequences of their actions. The deception that had shrouded the realm was exposed, unraveling the carefully crafted facade that once masked their misdeeds.

It was a watershed moment for the kingdom. The people, empowered by the truth, felt a newfound sense of liberation and unity. They pledged to stand together, vigilant against future deception and manipulation. The lessons learned from this tumultuous chapter would shape the collective consciousness, creating a society that values transparency, integrity, and the welfare of its citizens above all else.

In the aftermath of this period of reckoning, reforms were initiated to rebuild trust between the monarchy and its people. The King and his advisors took steps to acknowledge their mistakes, seeking to regain the confidence they had squandered. Policies were revised, accountability mechanisms were strengthened, and efforts were made to ensure that the voices of the people were heard and respected.

The kingdom emerged from this dark chapter with a newfound commitment to honesty and justice. The memory of the past served as a potent reminder of the fragility of power and the responsibility that comes with it. The once-angry populace, now emboldened by their collective strength, transformed into active participants in shaping the destiny of their nation.

King Awandit's tale and his kingdom's great awakening would be remembered for generations to come. It became a timeless reminder that truth and transparency are essential pillars of a just and stable society. From that moment onward, the people vowed never to let their voices be silenced, never to be deceived again, and forever to stand united to pursue a brighter future for all.

From that moment onward, Gotnhom once shrouded in the shadows of deceit and manipulation, experienced a truly extraordinary metamorphosis. The events catalyzed change, propelling the nation towards a brighter, more promising future. As the sun rose in this new era, it brought hope and a collective determination to rebuild the kingdom upon transparency, honesty, and genuine governance principles.

The emergence of new leaders was a testament to the resilience and strength of the people of Alek. These leaders, chosen by the populace for their integrity and vision, recognized the dire need for reform and embraced the immense responsibility ahead. With a deep understanding of the mistakes and suffering caused by the dark era of deception, they vowed to be the catalysts of positive change and healing.

The multifaceted transformation process involved

structural, institutional, and cultural shifts. The governance foundations were meticulously re-examined and reconstructed, with transparency becoming the cornerstone of every decision and action. Public trust, which had once been fractured, was now seen as the lifeblood of a functional and flourishing kingdom. The leaders made it their mission to ensure that the people had access to accurate information and that their voices were heard in shaping the nation's future.

Honesty became the guiding principle of communication between the government and its citizens. Gone were the days of half-truths and manipulative narratives, replaced by open dialogue and candid acknowledgment of challenges. Leaders understood that acknowledging mistakes and learning from them was vital to fostering a culture of growth and accountability.

The transformation extended beyond the corridors of power, permeating every aspect of society. Communities took it upon themselves to bridge the gaps that had once divided them, fostering unity and cooperation. Grassroots movements flourished, championing causes that reflected the collective aspirations and needs of the people. Citizens came together in solidarity, reinforcing that they held the power to shape their destiny.

Gotnhom's journey toward progress was challenging. Old habits and entrenched interests resisted the winds of change, but the lessons from the dark era served as a constant reminder of the high price of complacency. The people were vigilant, determined never to let history repeat itself. The scars of the past were not forgotten but transformed into a collective resolve to build a more just, inclusive, and compassionate society.

Over time, Gotnhom's remarkable transformation caught the international community's attention. The nation had become a shining example of how an indomitable spirit and genuine leadership could overcome even the most formidable obstacles. Diplomats, academics, and leaders from other nations sought to learn from Gotnhom's experiences, hoping to replicate its success and apply the invaluable lessons in their contexts.

From that pivotal moment forward, Gotnhom continued to evolve, with each generation cherishing the history that led them to this point. The journey was far from over, but the transformation had laid the groundwork for a future filled with promise and possibility. The power of the people was never underestimated again, as a constant reminder that unity and integrity could pave the way for a nation's ultimate triumph over darkness.

And so, the tale of deception in politics and governance weaved its way into the annals of history, etching itself as a cautionary tale for future generations. As time marched forward, the events that transpired in Gotnhom became a poignant reminder of the dangers that lurked when those in power strayed from the path of honesty and transparency.

The repercussions of this dark chapter echoed far and wide, touching the hearts and minds of citizens who vowed never to forget the lessons learned. The memory of these troubled times served as a rallying cry, urging the populace to remain vigilant and proactive in safeguarding the principles of democracy and good governance. The people of Gotnhom understood that democracy was not a guarantee but a delicate construct that required constant nurturing and protection.

In the wake of this turmoil, the citizens of Gotnhom found themselves encouraged to question authority, unyielding in their pursuit of truth, and unafraid to hold those in power accountable for their actions. The transparency and account-ability lacking in the past were now considered sacrosanct pillars of their society. The once complacent masses had transformed into a vigilant and informed populace, deter-mined to play an active role in shaping their destiny.

Alek emerged from this ordeal with a newfound under-standing that trust is not bestowed upon leaders automatically; it is earned through unwavering dedication to the welfare of the people they serve. The accurate measure of leader-ship was no longer confined to charismatic oratory skills, but rather it hinged upon integrity, empathy, and a genuine commitment to the betterment of society.

Gone were the days when the allure of charisma could blind the populace to the shortcomings of their leaders. The people demanded integrity, transparency, and a genuine desire to uplift the nation. The corridors of power resonated with a sense of responsibility that transcended personal ambition and embraced a collective vision for progress and prosperity.

As the years passed, Gotnhom witnessed a gradual trans-formation. The scars of deception were a constant reminder of the fragility of trust and the importance of upholding ethi-cal standards in governance. The nation's leaders understood that they were not above scrutiny and that their actions would be subject to the watchful eyes of an informed and engaged citizenry.

The legacy of this cautionary tale reached far beyond Gotnhom's borders, inspiring other nations to introspect and learn from their mistakes. It became a powerful parable for the world, emphasizing the value of democratic institutions, the significance of a responsible and vigilant citizenry, and the necessity of holding leaders accountable for their deeds.

And so, Gotnhom's journey from a dark period of deception to a brighter future of integrity and accountability became a beacon of hope for humanity. As long as the past lessons were etched into the collective memory, the tale would continue to serve as a timeless reminder of the importance of safeguarding the principles that underpin a just and prosperous society. The people of Gotnhom knew their shared history had forged a legacy that would endure for generations, guiding the path toward a more enlightened and harmonious world.

Chapter Six

The Internet and the Battle for Truth

I n the digital age, the Internet has undeniably emerged as an unprecedented and influential force, fundamentally transforming how we communicate, access information, and perceive the world around us. As this chapter delves into the multifaceted aspects of this digital landscape, we begin by shedding light on how the Internet functions as a double-edged sword, simultaneously exposing and perpetuating deception.

Social media platforms have become the epicenter of modern communication, connecting billions of people world-wide. On the one hand, they offer unparalleled opportunities for networking, sharing ideas, and disseminating information on a global scale. However, on the other hand, these platforms have amplified the dissemination of misinformation, making it easier for deceptive narratives to spread like wildfire[23]. The viral nature of sensational content often precedes accuracy and truth, leading to the rapid proliferation of falsehoods and misleading information.

One of the most concerning consequences of the Internet's influence is the rise of online echo chambers. These digital spaces consist of like-minded individuals who only interact with those who share similar beliefs and viewpoints. Echo chambers create an environment where people are continuously exposed to information that reaffirms their beliefs while shielding them from opposing perspectives. This reinforcement of preconceived notions can lead to increased polarization and hinder constructive dialogue, making it challenging for society to discern fact from fiction.

Moreover, the Internet has provided a fertile breeding ground for the proliferation of conspiracy theories. While these theories have always existed, the Internet's vast reach has given them an unprecedented platform to spread rapidly and gain traction. Conspiracy theories can be dangerous, sowing distrust in official narratives and institutions and potentially inciting harmful actions based on unfounded beliefs.

However, amid this digital landscape marred by deception and misinformation, the Internet has also empowered truth-seekers and fact-checkers to counter the spread of falsehoods. Online communities of individuals dedicated to verifying information and debunking conspiracy theories have emerged, striving to uncover hidden truths and disseminate accurate knowledge. These efforts have been instrumental in promoting critical thinking and encouraging a more discerning approach to consuming information.

Fact-checking organizations and independent journalists have embraced the Internet's potential to investigate claims, identify misinformation, and present evidence-based conclusions. These efforts are essential in the fight against deception, as they aim to restore trust in Reliable sources of information and promote a well-informed and educated society.

Additionally, technological advancements have enabled sophisticated algorithms and artificial intelligence tools to identify and flag misinformation. Social media platforms and search engines have addressed the issue by implementing fact-checking mechanisms and warning labels on potentially misleading content.

In conclusion, the Internet has undoubtedly revolutionized the way we interact with information and each other. While it has exposed and perpetuated deception through social media, echo chambers, and the spread of conspiracy theories, it has also empowered truth-seekers to counter misinformation and uncover hidden truths. As we navigate this digital era, balancing the freedom of information dissemination and the responsibility to ensure that accuracy and validity prevail in the virtual realm is crucial.

The Internet, a revolutionary technological marvel, has undeniably transformed how we live, work, and communicate. It has given humanity an unparalleled gift – the ability to access information from every corner of the globe, connecting people and cultures like never before. With its vast and open landscape, the Internet has become an indispensable tool in our daily lives, shaping our interactions, informing our decisions, and influencing our perspectives.

However, this digital utopia has not been without its challenges. As the Internet grew and interconnected individuals and societies, it also created a formidable battle for truth. Pursuing accurate information has become an arduous journey in this era, marked by the rapid dissemination of misinformation, fake news, and manipulated narratives. The essence of truth has been obscured, entangled within the virtual web of deceit and falsehoods.

The causes of this battle for truth on the Internet are multifaceted. Firstly, the ease of information sharing on online platforms has facilitated the spread of unverified or deliberately misleading content. With the click of a button, false information can be propagated to millions, leaving little time for critical analysis before it takes root in the minds of unsuspecting readers.

Secondly, the Internet's anonymity and freedom have given rise to malicious actors seeking to manipulate public opinion for their gain. These nefarious entities exploit the Internet's vastness to disseminate propaganda, sowing seeds of discord and confusion among the masses. Discerning fact from fiction becomes an arduous task in this chaotic digital realm.

Furthermore, social media platforms and algorithms often contribute to the amplification of misinformation. They may prioritize engaging or sensational content, regardless of its veracity, thus inadvertently fostering the spread of deceptive narratives. The echo chambers formed by these platforms can reinforce false beliefs and create insular communities, making it increasingly difficult to bridge the gap between differing perspectives.

The consequences of this battle for truth are profound and far-reaching. Misinformation can erode trust in institutions, sow division among communities, and undermine democratic processes. It can impact public health, influencing vaccination decisions, medical treatments, and crisis responses. Moreover, it can incite real-world violence and harm, as seen in instances of misinformation fueling social unrest and even contributing to acts of violence.

Addressing this complex issue requires collaborative efforts from various stakeholders. Technology companies must proactively curb the spread of misinformation by implementing robust fact-checking mechanisms, promoting media literacy, and refining algorithms to prioritize accuracy over sensationalism. Educators should integrate critical thinking and digital literacy skills into curricula, equipping the younger generation to responsibly navigate the vast information landscape.

Furthermore, media organizations and journalists are responsible for upholding rigorous journalistic standards, fact-checking rigorously before publishing, and promoting transparency to rebuild public trust in the media's role as a purveyor of truth.

As individuals, we must become conscious of information consumers, cultivating a healthy skepticism and verifying claims before accepting them as truth. Engaging in open, respectful dialogue with those holding different viewpoints can foster empathy and understanding, mitigating the effects of echo chambers.

Ultimately, the battle for truth on the Internet will persist as long as human nature seeks to exploit and deceive. Nevertheless, by acknowledging the challenges and working collectively towards fostering a culture of truth and accountability, we can harness the Internet's transformative power for the betterment of society. Pursuing accurate information in this digital age may be arduous. Still, it is a journey worth undertaking to safeguard the very fabric of truth that binds us together as a global community.

The advent of the Internet has been a transformative force in modern society, bringing tremendous opportunities and significant challenges. One of its most remarkable aspects is empowering individuals to become content creators, effectively democratizing information dissemination. With just an internet connection, people from all walks of life can now publish their thoughts, ideas, and expertise, breaking down traditional barriers that once limited access to information and knowledge. This newfound accessibility has sparked an era of unprecedented information-sharing, revolutionizing how we learn and interact with the world.

Undoubtedly, the democratization of information has had numerous positive impacts. It has provided a platform for marginalized voices and communities, allowing them to gain recognition and influence on a global scale. Niche interests and previously overlooked topics now have dedicated spaces where enthusiasts can connect and grow, fostering vibrant communities that might not have thrived in the pre-Internet era. From bloggers and vloggers to podcasters and social media influencers, countless individuals have leveraged the Internet's power to amplify their voices, challenging traditional media monopolies and introducing fresh perspectives into public discourse.

Furthermore, the Internet has become a vast repository of valuable knowledge, accessible at our fingertips. Educational resources, scholarly articles, and informative websites are readily available to anyone seeking to expand their understanding of virtually any subject. This wealth of information has revolutionized education, enabling individuals to independently engage in self-directed learning and explore their interests.

However, amid this wave of information empowerment lies an unsettling truth: the Internet's dual nature makes it a breeding ground for misinformation, deception, and manipulation. The sheer volume and ease of sharing information online create a prime environment for rapidly disseminating false or misleading content. Malicious actors and those with ill intentions exploit this vulnerability to spread disinformation, propaganda, and fake news, further muddying the truth.

Misinformation campaigns can have far-reaching consequences, ranging from undermining public trust in credible institutions and media to influencing political opinions and decision-making. The rise of "filter bubbles" and echo chambers, where individuals are only exposed to information that aligns with their existing beliefs, exacerbates this problem, as it limits critical thinking and fosters confirmation bias.

Moreover, the digital age has introduced new challenges when verifying the authenticity of information. Deepfakes and other sophisticated manipulations make it increasingly difficult to discern real from fake, blurring the line between truth and fiction. In such an environment, individuals are responsible for developing media literacy skills and critically evaluating the sources and credibility of the information they encounter.

As the Internet continues to evolve, striking a balance between preserving the open exchange of ideas and curbing the spread of misinformation remains a complex challenge. Technological advancements, improved media literacy efforts, and responsible content moderation are essential in mitigating the negative impacts of deceptive information. Likewise, promoting digital citizenship and critical thinking among internet users can help foster a more discerning online community, less susceptible to manipulation and misinformation.

In conclusion, the Internet is indeed a double-edged sword. On the one hand, it has empowered individuals to become content creators and democratized information, revolutionizing how we access and share knowledge. However, on the other hand, the ease of information dissemination has given rise to the proliferation of misleading and false content, posing significant challenges to societal trust and the reliability of information. Navigating these complexities requires a collective effort from individuals, technology companies, educators, and policymakers to ensure that the Internet remains a force for positive change while guarding against its potential to harm and mislead.

The Rise of Misinformation

In recent years, the proliferation of misinformation, defined as intentionally or unintentionally false or misleading information, has reached alarming heights, permeating virtually every corner of the Internet with their unprecedented reach, social media platforms, have emerged as key contributors to the rapid dissemination of misinformation, propagating its reach to millions of users within moments[24,25]. This escalating trend has far-reaching consequences, casting profound shadows over public opinion, political landscapes, and public health initiatives.

At the heart of this crisis lies the unprecedented connectivity and accessibility facilitated by the Internet and social media platforms. While these technological advancements have undoubtedly enriched human interactions and global connectivity, they have also become breeding grounds for the viral spread of unverified, misleading, or false information. The viral nature of misinformation is fueled by powerful algorithms employed by social media platforms, which often prioritize sensational content over accuracy. This creates echo chambers where users are exposed to information reinforcing their beliefs, inadvertently supporting the echo chamber effect, and making them susceptible to even more misinformation.

Public opinion, which forms the backbone of democratic societies, has suffered a significant blow due to the proliferation of misinformation. Misleading narratives and fabricated stories can sway public sentiment, leading to misunderstandings, mistrust, and the erosion of societal harmony. Furthermore, misinformation has insidiously crept into political discourse, influencing election outcomes, and undermining the foundation of democratic processes. The spread of false information can manipulate voters, distort facts, and alter electoral results, posing a severe threat to the principles of fair governance.

Even more concerning is the impact misinformation has had on public health. The outbreak of the COVID-19 pandemic in recent years demonstrated how quickly false information can spread and exacerbate a global health crisis. Misinformation surrounding the virus's origins, transmission, and potential cures hindered effective public health responses, jeopardizing lives, and hindering efforts to control the pandemic. In such situations, believing and sharing misinformation can be dire, undermining trust in reputable health authorities and scientific expertise[26].

Addressing the rise of misinformation requires a multifaceted approach involving various stakeholders, including technology companies, governments, educators, and individuals. Social media platforms must take more robust measures to identify and remove false information while promoting credible sources. Algorithmic transparency and responsible content curation are crucial steps toward mitigating the spread of misinformation.

Educational institutions should prioritize media literacy, equipping individuals with the skills to evaluate information and discern reliable sources from deceptive ones critically.

Empowering users to question the integrity of information they encounter can act as a powerful deterrent again the spreading of misinformation.

Governments also play a pivotal role in countering misinformation. They can enact legislation that holds tech companies accountable for their role in disseminating false information while also supporting initiatives that promote fact-checking and accurate reporting.

Finally, individuals must adopt a vigilant and responsible approach to information consumption. Being mindful of the sources, corroborating facts, and avoiding the hasty sharing of unverified information can help curb misinformation's virality.

The rise of misinformation is an enduring challenge that demands immediate attention and concerted efforts from all sectors of society. By embracing responsibility, promoting media literacy, and prioritizing truth, we can reclaim the integrity of information and build a more informed, enlightened digital world. Only through collective action can we counter the rampant spread of misinformation and safeguard the future of our interconnected society.

Echo Chambers and Confirmation Bias

The Internet has undoubtedly revolutionized the way we access information and interact with one another. It has facilitated the swift dissemination of knowledge, bringing diverse perspectives and ideas to our fingertips. However, amidst this vast sea of information lies a phenomenon that threatens the essence of truth-seeking and understanding: the formation of echo chambers and the reinforcement of confirmation bias.

In the virtual realm, like-minded individuals have found solace in creating online communities called echo chambers. These digital spaces offer a sense of belonging and validation, as individuals can interact with others who share their beliefs and viewpoints. While seeking like-minded people is natural human behavior, the Internet has magnified this tendency, making it easier to find and connect with others who validate our opinions, sometimes without any critical evaluation.

As users navigate the online landscape, they unwittingly encounter algorithms designed to personalize content based on their preferences and past behaviors. These algorithms, often used by social media platforms, search engines, and recommendation systems, aim to keep users engaged by presenting information that aligns with their preexisting opinions and interests. This personalized content may seem innocuous, catering to users' preferences and providing relevant information. However, its implications are more profound and far-reaching than meets the eye.

Confirmation bias, a cognitive bias where individuals tend to interpret and favor information that confirms their existing beliefs while ignoring or dismissing contradictory evidence, comes into play in these digital realms. Users are continuously exposed to content that reinforces their views, so they become increasingly entrenched in their beliefs. This narrow perspective hinders the pursuit of truth and fosters societal polarization and divisiveness[27].

The consequences of echo chambers and confirmation bias are alarming. Instead of engaging in healthy debates and constructive dialogue, individuals within these digital enclaves become resistant to new ideas and alternative viewpoints. Critical thinking takes a backseat as emotions and beliefs precede facts and evidence. As a result, genuine understanding and cooperation become increasingly challenging to achieve, leading to heightened social and political polarization.

The echo chamber phenomenon also threatens the credibility of information sources. Misinformation and disinformation spread like wildfire within these closed communities, where dubious claims go unchallenged and gain unwarranted credibility. This perpetuates an environment where rumors, conspiracy theories, and falsehoods thrive, further blurring the line between fact and fiction.

We must actively strive for a more balanced and open information ecosystem to combat the adverse effects of echo chambers and confirmation bias. Individuals should be encouraged to seek diverse viewpoints, think critically, and question their beliefs. Furthermore, online platforms and technology companies are responsible for designing algorithms prioritizing information accuracy and diversity over mere personalization.

The Internet is a powerful tool that has the potential to unite and enlighten humanity, but it requires responsible use and thoughtful design. By recognizing the dangers of echo chambers and confirmation bias, we can promote intellectual curiosity, empathy, and a shared commitment to truth, ultimately fostering a more informed, tolerant, and united global society.

Manipulation and Disinformation Campaigns

In the digital era, the Internet has become a powerful tool connecting billions of people across the globe. While it has undoubtedly brought positive advancements, it has also opened doors for a darker side to emerge. State and non-state actors have ingeniously harnessed the vast potential of the online world to orchestrate insidious disinformation campaigns, plunging society into an era of distrust and bewilderment[28].

The web of deception begins with the deliberate dissemination of false narratives. Armed with cunning agendas, these actors manipulate and distort information, fabricating stories that align with their vested interests. Whether it be political, economic, or ideological motives, their end goal is to manipulate public opinion and incite division within communities. The viral nature of the Internet accelerates the spread of these falsehoods, making it challenging for the truth to prevail.

Exploiting the interconnectedness of the digital realm, these adversaries manipulate online discussions with an artistry that disguises their intentions. They infiltrate social media platforms, forums, and comment sections, amplifying certain viewpoints while suppressing others. By strategically deploying an army of bots and fake accounts, they create the illusion of widespread support for their narratives, ultimately influencing the beliefs and actions of unsuspecting users.

Beyond merely sowing seeds of confusion, these evil forces resort to more aggressive tactics, infiltrating sensitive systems through cyberattacks. With their mastery over hacking techniques, they breach organizational networks, compromising data and launching destructive attacks. Their willingness to breach digital boundaries poses a formidable challenge to cybersecurity and threatens the stability of institutions that society relies upon.

The implications of these campaigns are profound, eroding the very foundations of truth and public trust. Citizens are left questioning the credibility of information sources, trying to figure out what to believe amidst the deluge of conflicting narratives. The lines between fact and fiction blur, leaving society vulnerable to the sway of manipulative forces.

Consequently, the integrity of information is severely compromised. In this post-truth era, the erosion of public trust in institutions, media, and each other hampers societal cohesion. Polarization ensues as people retreat into echo chambers that reinforce their preconceived notions, further deepening societal divisions.

Addressing this menace requires a multifaceted approach. Governments, tech companies, and civil society must collaborate to develop robust strategies to counter disinformation. Enhancing media literacy education can empower citizens to discern credible sources and detect falsehoods. Furthermore, social media platforms should fortify their defenses against fake accounts and automated bots while promoting advertising and content moderation transparency.

Safeguarding the integrity of the Internet and rebuilding

public trust is a collective responsibility. By recognizing the perni-
cious influence of manipulation and disinformation campaigns,
society can strive for a more informed and united future where
the Internet remains a force for good rather than a weapon for
deception and chaos. We can only navigate the treacherous
waters of the digital age and emerge stronger, wiser, and more
resilient through collective vigilance and action.

Combating the Battle for Truth

Addressing the battle for truth on the Internet requires a
multifaceted approach involving technological, educational,
and societal interventions. In the digital age, the spread of
information has become easier and faster than ever before.
However, this unprecedented accessibility has also given rise
to a concerning challenge: the battle for truth. Misinformation,
fake news, and disinformation have infiltrated online platforms, sowing confusion, dividing societies, and eroding
trust in reliable sources of information. To effectively tackle
this issue, a comprehensive strategy encompassing various
dimensions of society is crucial. These strategies include:

1. Technological Interventions: Advancements in technology have enabled the rapid dissemination of information but
have also facilitated the spread of falsehoods. Technology
can play a significant role in combating the battle for truth.
This involves developing and implementing advanced algorithms and artificial intelligence (AI) systems to identify and

flag misleading content. Social media platforms and search engines can utilize such tools to reduce the visibility of misinformation and prioritize credible sources.

Furthermore, collaborations between tech companies and fact-checking organizations can be established to verify information and label disputed content. Employing cryptographic techniques and blockchain technology may also help create a more transparent and immutable record of the information's origin and integrity.

2. Educational Initiatives: Promoting media literacy and critical thinking skills is essential in the fight against misinformation. Educational institutions should integrate media literacy programs into their curricula, starting from early education levels. These programs can teach students how to discern credible sources, fact-check information, and critically analyze online content. By equipping individuals with the ability to evaluate information objectively, they become less susceptible to manipulation and misinformation.

Public awareness campaigns targeting all age groups can also emphasize the importance of verifying information before sharing it. Encouraging a culture of responsible information sharing can substantially reduce the spread of false or misleading content.

3. Societal Interventions: The battle for truth is not solely a technological or educational issue; it also involves societal dynamics. Governments, civil society organizations, and individuals must actively participate in fostering an environment where truth is valued and promoted. Policymakers can enact legislation to hold platforms accountable for hosting false information while safeguarding freedom of speech and expression.

Media organizations should adhere to high journalistic standards and prioritize fact-based reporting. Encouraging media outlets to present balanced perspectives and verify information before publishing can enhance the overall credibility of news sources.

Furthermore, fostering open and constructive dialogues among diverse communities can help bridge ideological gaps and reduce the polarization that often accompanies the spread of misinformation. Promoting empathy, respect, and tolerance for differing viewpoints can lead to a more united and informed society.

4. Collaborative Efforts: Collaborative efforts stand as a pivotal force in addressing the challenge of misinformation and promoting accuracy in information dissemination. This cooperative approach brings together a diverse array of stakeholders, including governments, technology companies, educators, civil society organizations, and individuals, each contributing their unique expertise and resources to combat falsehoods. The synergy created by this collective endeavour yields a multifaceted response to the complex issue of misinformation.

Through collaborative efforts, a broad spectrum of expertise converges to counter the spread of falsehoods. Fact-checkers, researchers, journalists, and psychologists collaborate to scrutinize and debunk inaccuracies, ensuring a well-rounded assessment of the information landscape. Moreover, resource sharing among participants enhances preparedness by pooling financial backing, technological innovations, data analytics tools, and communication networks. This shared pool of resources fosters a comprehensive and robust strategy to tackle the challenges posed by deceptive content across various platforms and languages.

Collaborative endeavours also leverage the strengths of different sectors to address misinformation comprehensively. Governments enact policies, technology companies develop algorithms, educators promote media literacy, civil society organizations run awareness campaigns, and individuals engage in responsible information sharing. By coordinating efforts and sharing insights, stakeholders remain adaptable and ahead of evolving misinformation tactics. This collective approach not only ensures mutual accountability but also magnifies the impact of campaigns and initiatives, fostering informed societies that are resilient to the harmful effects of misinformation.

5. Governments: Governments play a pivotal role in shaping the landscape of information dissemination by wielding their authority to establish and enforce regulations that foster a climate of transparency, accountability, and integrity. Through the formulation of comprehensive policies, governments can set the tone for truthfulness in media and online platforms. By requiring accurate sourcing, fact-checking, and clear labelling of content, they can empower citizens to make informed decisions and cultivate a more trustworthy information ecosystem. Furthermore, governments can allocate resources towards initiatives aimed at curbing the spread of misinformation, both domestically and across borders. Collaborative efforts with international counterparts can result in a unified front against disinformation, safeguarding not only the integrity of their own societies but also promoting global stability in an era where information transcends geographical boundaries.

In a digital age where misinformation can proliferate rapidly, governments hold the responsibility of creating an environment that promotes the reliability of information. This entails not only enacting regulations but also fostering partnerships with media organizations, tech companies, and civil society groups. By supporting research, educational campaigns, and media literacy programs, governments can equip individuals with the critical thinking skills necessary to discern accurate information from falsehoods. Striking a balance between regulation and safeguarding freedom of expression is a challenge government must navigate adeptly. A transparent and consultative approach to policymaking ensures that the diverse needs of society are considered, reinforcing the public's trust in institutions. Ultimately, governments serve as linchpins in the fight against misinformation, using their authority to mold a reality where accurate information is not only championed but is the foundation upon which societies thrive.

6. **Technology Companies:** In today's interconnected world, the influence of technology companies on information

dissemination cannot be overstated. These companies have become the gatekeepers of information, shaping how news, ideas, and opinions are spread across the digital landscape. With this influence comes a distinct responsibility to ensure the accuracy and credibility of the content being disseminated. By forging partnerships with technology companies, a collaborative effort can be initiated to tackle the complex challenge of misinformation. By enhancing content moderation systems, these companies can weed out false or misleading information before it gains widespread traction. Moreover, technology firms have the potential to utilize their advanced algorithms to promote reliable and well-established sources of information, giving users access to content that is backed by research and expertise. Addressing algorithmic biases is equally paramount, as unintentional biases can exacerbate the spread of misinformation by reinforcing pre-existing beliefs. Through these combined efforts, technology companies can harness their capabilities to build a digital landscape that fosters accurate, unbiased, and trustworthy information flow.

Nonetheless, the role of technology companies in combating misinformation requires careful balance. While these companies possess the tools to influence the flow of information, they must also respect principles of free speech and avoid becoming arbiters of truth. Collaborative efforts should prioritize transparency and inclusivity, engaging experts, scholars, and civil society to collectively define standards for content moderation and source credibility. The responsibility goes beyond mere technological fixes – it encompasses the creation of an informed digital society. As technology companies work to refine their algorithms and content ranking systems, they should be conscious of the potential of unintended consequences, such as echo chambers and filter bubbles. Striking this balance requires ongoing dialogue, research, and adaptability, as the landscape of information dissemination and technology continues to evolve. In essence, the collaboration between technology companies and other stakeholders holds the promise of nurturing an online environment that empowers individuals with accurate knowledge while preserving the democratic ideals of open discourse and diverse perspectives.

7. Educators: Educators hold a pivotal role in shaping the intellectual landscape of the future by nurturing critical thinking skills and promoting media literacy. In a world where information is abundantly available and misinformation can easily proliferate, educators become the guiding lights for students seeking to navigate this intricate digital realm. By seamlessly integrating media literacy education into curricula, educators provide students with the essential tools to differentiate between credible sources and deceptive content. Through thoughtfully designed lessons, students learn to question, analyse, and cross-reference information, ultimately honing their ability to distinguish truth from falsehood. This not only safeguards them against falling prey to misinformation but also cultivates a sense of responsibility in assessing information before accepting it at face value. As educators encourage a healthy skepticism and an appetite for inquiry, they lay the foundation for a generation that critically engages with the world, making well-informed decisions that shape societies for the better.

With media literacy as a cornerstone of education, educators instill in students the competence to interpret and evaluate media messages with discernment. By dissecting various media forms such as news articles, social media posts, videos, and advertisements, students learn to recognize biased narratives, sensationalism, and manipulation tactics that can distort reality. This empowers them to become active participants in a democratic society, capable of contributing constructively to public discourse and holding institutions accountable. Moreover, media literacy education equips students to not only consume media mindfully but also to create content ethically and responsibly. By understanding the impact of their words and visuals, students develop a heightened awareness of their digital footprint and the potential influence they can wield. In this way, educators serve as catalysts for the development of a media-literate populace that critically engages with information, challenges prevailing narratives, and fosters a culture of integrity and authenticity in communication.

8. Civil Society Organizations (CSO): Civil Society Organizations play a pivotal role in safeguarding the integrity of information in today's digital age. As non-governmental entities driven by a commitment to social betterment, CSOs possess the unique ability to act as vigilant watchdogs against the proliferation of misinformation. By monitoring various sources of information and utilizing their networks, these organizations can swiftly identify and expose misleading content, thus preventing its harmful consequences from taking root. Their dedication to transparency and truthfulness compels them to hold both individuals and institutions accountable for the information they share, helping to maintain the quality and accuracy of public discourse.

Moreover, CSOs can exert a significant impact by fostering partnerships with independent fact-checking organizations. In an era where the volume of information overwhelms the average user, fact-checkers serve as a vital line of defense against the spread of falsehoods. Civil society groups can provide financial and logistical support to these fact-checkers, enabling them to rigorously investigate claims, verify sources, and present evidence-based findings to the public. By collaborating with these organizations, CSOs leverage their collective strength to counteract the influence of misinformation, ensuring that reliable information takes precedence in shaping public opinions and decisions. This synergy between CSOs and fact-checkers exemplifies the potential for a multi-faceted approach to truth preservation in the digital age.

In essence, the involvement of CSO in combating misinformation embodies the principles of civic engagement and social responsibility. By wielding their influence to raise awareness, challenge falsehoods, and support independent fact-checking efforts, CSOs contribute to the maintenance of an informed and empowered society. In a time when misinformation can spread rapidly through online platforms, the active participation of these organizations serves as a crucial bulwark against the erosion of truth and the manipulation of public discourse.

9. Individuals: In the modern age of information overload, empowering individuals as discerning consumers of information is an indispensable step in the ongoing battle for truth. The rapid proliferation of digital platforms and social media has given rise to a plethora of information sources, making it increasingly challenging to distinguish between reliable facts and misleading content. By promoting media literacy and fostering critical thinking skills among the public, societies can equip individuals with the tools they need to navigate this complex landscape. Media literacy entails teaching individuals how to analyse the credibility of sources, assess the accuracy of information, and recognize potential biases. Armed with these skills, people can become more adept at identifying misinformation and disinformation, thereby curbing the unwitting spread of false narratives. When individuals approach information with a critical eye, they become less susceptible to manipulation and are better positioned to make informed decisions, contributing to the cultivation of an informed and truth-seeking society.

Encouraging media literacy and critical thinking doesn't solely benefit individuals; it has a cascading effect that ripples through society. As more people gain the ability to differentiate between trustworthy information and dubious claims, the overall demand for reliable and accurate content increases. This shift in demand incentivizes media organizations to prioritize responsible journalism, focusing on well-researched stories backed by credible sources. Consequently, the spread of misinformation is constrained, as the market for sensationalism and falsehoods diminishes. Moreover, a populace equipped with critical thinking skills becomes less vulnerable to the divisive tactics of malicious actors seeking to sow discord by exploiting information gaps. By nurturing a culture of skepticism and intellectual curiosity, societies fortify their resilience against the manipulation of truth. Ultimately, the empowerment of individuals as vigilant information consumers becomes a formidable defense against the erosion of truth in the digital age.

10. Sharing Best Practices: In the realm of combating misinformation, the essence of collaborative efforts lies in the sharing of successful strategies and best practices among diverse stakeholders. Governments, recognizing the global nature of the challenge, can glean valuable insights from the experiences of other countries. By examining the successes and failures of various approaches, they can fine-tune their own tactics and policies to better address the complexities of misinformation. This cross-border learning not only facilitates the adoption of proven methods but also sparks innovation as nations adapt and customize strategies to suit their unique socio-political contexts. Furthermore, this collaborative exchange encourages diplomatic dialogue and cooperation, promoting a collective commitment to truth and information integrity on an international scale.

Equally pivotal in this collaborative ecosystem are technology companies, which play a crucial role in shaping the online landscape. These entities can share effective content moderation techniques that have proven instrumental in countering misinformation. By pooling their collective knowledge, technology companies can refine algorithms, implement stringent fact-checking mechanisms, and develop cutting-edge tools that identify and mitigate the spread of false information. Through partnerships with academia and research institutions, they can harness the power of artificial intelligence and machine learning to proactively detect patterns of misinformation, ultimately safeguarding digital spaces from manipulation. This knowledge-sharing fosters a dynamic cycle of continuous improvement, where platforms constantly evolve their defenses against misinformation, staying one step ahead of ever-adapting misinformation tactics.

11. Supporting Independent Fact-Checking Organizations: Supporting Independent Fact-Checking Organizations is an essential pillar in the battle against misinformation and the erosion of trust in public discourse. These organizations function as the watchdogs of truth, meticulously investigating claims and scrutinizing information to determine their accuracy. By collaborating with such fact-checking entities, societies can foster a culture of critical thinking and informed decision-making. The role of these organizations extends beyond mere verification; they serve as beacons of transparency, offering a counterbalance to the overwhelming tide of unverified and false information that often pervades social media platforms and news outlets. In an age where the speed of information dissemination has reached unprecedented levels, fact-checkers provide a vital layer of defense, helping to prevent the amplification of misleading or harmful content. By supporting these organizations, we not only uphold the integrity of information but also empower individuals to make well-informed choices based on verified and accurate data.

Collaboration with independent fact-checking organizations is not just about dispelling false claims; it's about fostering a sense of responsibility and accountability in information sharing. In an era where misinformation can spread rapidly and widely, these organizations function as a buffer against the distortion of reality. Their work reverberates across various domains, from politics to health to science, providing a solid foundation for public discourse and decision-making. By supporting independent fact-checkers, societies demonstrate a commitment to intellectual integrity and the pursuit of truth. Moreover, this collaboration serves as a reminder that the battle against misinformation is not a solitary endeavour, but a collective responsibility shared by governments, media, and individuals alike. The continued growth and influence of fact-checking organizations can lead to a more informed and vigilant society, where the veracity of information is paramount, and informed citizens are better equipped to navigate the complexities of our information-rich world.

12. Promoting Cross-Platform Cooperation: Promoting Cross-Platform Cooperation is a pivotal step in combating the rampant issue of misinformation that traverses numerous platforms and social media networks. In today's interconnected digital landscape, disinformation can swiftly spread like wild-fire, transcending the boundaries of individual platforms. By fostering collaboration among stakeholders, including social media companies, fact-checking organizations, researchers, and government agencies, a united front can be established against the dissemination of false information. This approach enables the pooling of resources, expertise, and technology, creating a more effective and streamlined response to the rapid spread of disinformation. Through joint efforts, stake-holders can share data, identify emerging trends, and develop innovative tools that can identify and mitigate false content across various platforms, thereby curtailing its virality.

Cross-platform cooperation not only enhances the speed of response but also enhances the accuracy of information verification. Different platforms possess varying capabilities and algorithms for detecting and moderating content, making collaboration essential to bridge these gaps. By working together, stakeholders can collectively develop best prac-tices and guidelines for identifying misinformation, ensuring consistency in tackling the issue across diverse platforms. Furthermore, this collaborative approach promotes trans-parency and accountability, as the shared responsibility for addressing misinformation encourages platforms to proac-tively implement measures that curtail its reach. Overall, promoting cross-platform cooperation acts as a force multi-plier in the fight against misinformation, leveraging the strengths of multiple stakeholders to create a more resilient and comprehensive defense against its harmful effects.

In conclusion, the complexity and speed of information

dissemination in the digital age necessitate a multifaceted approach to tackling misinformation. Promoting cross-platform cooperation empowers stakeholders to collaborate across boundaries and disciplines, harnessing collective expertise to swiftly identify, verify, and counter false information. By fostering partnerships among social media networks, fact-checking organizations, researchers, and governments, a cohesive strategy emerges to combat the virulent spread of misinformation, fostering a more informed and discerning online community.

13. Enhancing Collective Efforts: The imperative to counteract misinformation in today's information-rich landscape underscores the significance of fostering collaboration among groups of stakeholders. By bringing together governments, technology companies, educators, civil society organizations, and individuals, a unified front emerges that possesses the potential to curtail the proliferation of falsehoods. The cooperation of their collective efforts not only fortifies the battle against misinformation but also imbues it with resilience, efficiency, and a more profound impact. As these diverse entities pool their resources, expertise, and insights, they form a formidable defense against the distortions that can erode public discourse, sow confusion, and undermine trust in institutions. Coordinated actions allow for a harmonized response that can detect and counteract misinformation across a range of platforms, languages, and formats. Moreover, this collaborative approach enables the crafting of comprehensive strategies encompassing fact-checking initiatives, algorithmic enhancements, media literacy programs, and regulatory measures. In a world where the rapid dissemination of information can either foster understanding or breed confusion, the enhancement of collective efforts is paramount to cultivating an informed and discerning society.

In conclusion, the multifaceted battle for truth requires the concerted endeavour of an interwoven tapestry of stakeholders. Governments, equipped with regulatory frameworks and enforcement mechanisms, can set standards that mitigate the spread of misinformation and ensure accountability. Technology companies, armed with advanced algorithms and content moderation tools, play a pivotal role in identifying and restricting the amplification of false information on digital platforms. Educators, through comprehensive media literacy programs, empower individuals with the critical thinking skills necessary to navigate the intricate web of information sources. Civil society organizations, driven by a commitment to accurate information dissemination, serve as watchdogs and advocates for responsible communication. Finally, individuals, armed with a heightened awareness of misinformation's pitfalls, become vigilant purveyors of accurate information within their social circles. In this holistic alliance, these distinct forces converge to foster a robust, unified response that not only counters misinformation but also cultivates a more enlightened and trustworthy information ecosystem for present and future generations.

Chapter Seven:
Environmental Truths and Denial

T he battle between truth and deception is not limited to individual beliefs or isolated incidents; it extends its ominous influence on the very health and well-being of our planet. In this chapter, we embark on a profound journey that delves into the heart of the clash between irrefutable scientific evidence on pressing environmental issues and the calculated denial propagated by vested interests with their agendas.

At the forefront of this fierce conflict lies the contentious issue of climate change. The scientific community has been unequivocal in its findings, presenting a substantial body of evidence indicating that human activities, especially burning fossil fuels, significantly contribute to the warming of the Earth's climate. Despite the overwhelming consensus among experts, powerful entities, driven by financial gains or political motives, choose to dismiss or downplay the reality of climate change. This denial not only obstructs meaningful action but also jeopardizes the future of our planet and the generations to come.

The repercussions of this clash between truth and deception reverberate across the spectrum of environmental concerns, particularly evident in the alarming rates of biodiversity loss. Scientists have diligently documented the disturbing decline in animal and plant species across diverse ecosystems, underscoring the detrimental impact of human activities such as habitat destruction, pollution, and overexploitation. However, vested interests with economic stakes in industries that contribute to this degradation often resort to obfuscation and denial, putting their short-term gains ahead of our planet's long-term ecological stability and resilience.

This dangerous confrontation between scientific reality and orchestrated deception exposes the fragility of our ecosystems and the delicate balance that sustains life on Earth. By refusing to acknowledge the integrity of scientific evidence, those who prioritize their narrow interests ignore the impending crisis that threatens global ecological systems. The consequences of denying reality in favour of immediate profits come at a steep cost to our natural world and human societies and economies.

As we venture further into this chapter, we shall witness the harrowing effects of this denial on both a local and global scale. We will uncover compelling stories of communities grappling with the adverse impacts of environmental degradation while seeking solutions despite resistance from those with vested interests. Moreover, we will explore the vital role of education, advocacy, and collective action in combating this deceptive narrative, ultimately advocating for sustainable policies and practices to safeguard our planet's health and secure a brighter future for all.

Environmental truths and denial are not isolated occurrences; they are deeply interconnected phenomena that carry far-reaching consequences for our planet and its inhabitants. With the global community confronting unparalleled challenges concerning climate change, pollution, deforestation, and the depletion of natural resources, it is of utmost importance to recognize and confront these realities. Only through acceptance and action can we secure future generations' well-being and the Earth's health[30,31].

One of the undeniable environmental truths is the escalating impact of climate change. The overwhelming scientific consensus demonstrates that human activities, particularly the emission of greenhouse gases, have led to the warming of our planet. The consequences are widespread and alarming, from more frequent and intense extreme weather events to rising sea levels threatening coastal communities. Failure to acknowledge this reality prolongs inaction and exacerbates the threats to vulnerable ecosystems and populations.

Pollution is another pressing truth we must confront. Human activities release vast quantities of pollutants into the air, water, and soil, causing severe damage to ecosystems and posing grave risks to human health. Toxic chemicals, plastic waste, and industrial emissions contaminate environments, affecting wildlife and entering the food chain. Denying the extent and impact of pollution only perpetuates its hazardous consequences and hampers the development of practical solutions.

Deforestation, a significant contributor to climate change, is yet another critical environmental truth. Forests act as essential carbon sinks, absorbing vast amounts of CO_2, but rampant deforestation diminishes this capacity, contributing to the accumulation of greenhouse gases. Moreover, forests are vital habitats for countless species, and their destruction disrupts entire ecosystems. Recognizing and addressing this truth entails safeguarding forests, promoting sustainable logging practices, and reforestation efforts.

The depletion of natural resources poses a fundamental challenge to human civilization. From fossil fuels to freshwater reserves, human consumption often exceeds the Earth's capacity to replenish these resources. Denying this reality and continuing with unsustainable exploitation further strains the planet's ability to support life, leading to resource scarcity, social unrest, and geopolitical tensions.

Addressing these environmental truths is not merely an altruistic endeavor; it is a necessity for the survival and prosperity of humanity. Embracing renewable energy sources, transitioning to more sustainable production and consumption patterns, and investing in green technologies are crucial steps to mitigate the damage we've caused and ensure a healthier, more resilient future.

The consequences of environmental denial can be catastrophic. Ignoring these realities perpetuates destructive behaviors, stifles progress, and widens the gap between those who understand the urgency of change and those who resist it. Overcoming denial requires education, awareness, and responsible leadership to drive collective action and create a sustainable path.

By acknowledging these truths and taking proactive steps to address them, we can pave the way for a more harmonious relationship between humanity and nature. This means engaging in international cooperation, enacting effective policies, and fostering a culture that values the preservation of the environment for future generations. Only through these concerted efforts can we forge a more promising future where the planet thrives, and its inhabitant's flourish. The time to act is now, and by embracing these truths, we can embark on a journey toward a greener, more sustainable world.

Environmental truths encompass a broad spectrum of irrefutable scientific evidence highlighting the alarming degradation of the Earth's delicate ecosystems and the perturbing shifts in its climate patterns. These truths are firmly rooted in rigorous research, comprehensive data analysis, and meticulous observations from diverse climatology, ecology, and environmental sciences disciplines. As we delve into this compelling realm of knowledge, several crucial environmental truths come to the forefront, revealing the precarious state of our planet and the urgent need for action[32].

Truths About Climate Change

1. Climate Change is Real and Accelerating: The irrefutable reality of climate change is indisputable, and its pace is quickening. Human actions, predominantly the release of greenhouse gases, constitute a significant driving force behind this transformative shift in the Earth's climate. This is starkly evident in the unprecedented surge in global temperatures, which has far-reaching consequences such as the escalating rise in sea levels, the intensification of extreme weather phenomena, and the widespread perturbation of ecosystems on a global scale. The cumulative impact of these changes serves as an undeniable testament to the urgent need for concerted efforts to mitigate further damage and secure a sustainable future for our planet.

2. Biodiversity Loss is a Crisis: Biodiversity loss stands as an urgent and formidable crisis, transcending geographical borders, as a multitude of species vanish with disconcerting rapidity due to the intertwined impacts of habitat degradation, pervasive pollution, unchecked overexploitation, and the overarching specter of climate change. This disintegration of diversity not only jeopardizes the intricate interplay of species within ecosystems but also casts a perilous shadow over the very fabric of human existence. The unraveling of this delicate tapestry imperils the stability and resilience of ecosystems that have thrived for millennia, placing in jeopardy not only the survival of countless irreplaceable organisms but also the elaborate web of life that sustains us all.

3. Human Impact is Widespread: The pervasive footprint of human influence is evident through a myriad of actions encompassing deforestation, rapid industrialization, and the intensive reshaping of agricultural practices. These collective endeavors have yielded profound transformations in once-pristine landscapes, leading to the unfortunate erosion of habitats and the insidious encroachment of environmental deterioration. In light of this, acknowledging the far-reaching consequences of our actions becomes imperative, as does the implementation of effective measures to curtail and reverse these negative effects. Only through a concerted commitment to recognizing and rectifying our impact can we hope to forge a pathway towards a future characterized by sustainability and harmony with the natural world.

4. Oceans are Under Threat: The world's oceans stand at a critical juncture, besieged by a convergence of grave challenges that cast a shadow over their very existence. The pervasive scourge of plastic pollution, a testament to humanity's throwaway culture, chokes the once-pristine waters and imperils countless marine species. Overfishing, driven by insatiable demand, disrupts the delicate balance of aquatic ecosystems, pushing some species to the brink of extinction and unsettling the intricate web of life that sustains our oceans. Adding to this turmoil, the relentless absorption of carbon dioxide leads to insidious ocean acidification, unraveling the beautiful life of coral reefs and cascading through the marine food chain. As these threats escalate, the survival of marine life hangs in the balance, casting a foreboding shadow over the millions whose livelihoods are intertwined with the health of the oceans. Urgent and concerted action is imperative, for the oceans' fate is inextricably linked to our own, and the time to reverse this tide of destruction is running perilously short.

5. Freshwater Resources are Scarce: The scarcity of freshwater resources is an escalating global concern, as the finite reserves of clean water are being steadily depleted in the face of mounting challenges such as pollution, excessive utilization, and the unrelenting impacts of climate change. This critical situation not only imperils the delicate balance of ecosystems but also casts a shadow of peril over human communities worldwide. Pollution from industrial, agricultural, and domestic sources continues to contaminate water bodies, rendering them unsuitable for consumption and jeopardizing aquatic life. Concurrently, the excessive demand for water, driven by burgeoning populations and escalating urbanization, strains available resources to their limits. The compounding effects of these challenges are exacerbated by the altering climate patterns, leading to erratic precipitation, prolonged droughts, and uncertain water availability. Consequently, the scarcity of freshwater not only disrupts delicate ecosystems but also poses a profound threat to human societies, underscoring the urgent need for collective action to conserve and judiciously manage this irreplaceable resource.

6. Deforestation is a Critical Issue: Deforestation stands as a critical and urgent issue that reverberates through our planet's intricate web of life. The extensive and relentless clearance of forests, driven by the voracious demands of agriculture, logging, and urban expansion, bears profound consequences that ripple across both space and time. The serious implications of this environmental tragedy extend to the very core of our climate stability, as trees play a crucial role in absorbing carbon dioxide, a key driver of global warming. Concurrently, the relentless felling of these arboreal havens also serves as a harbinger of biodiversity loss, as countless species teeter on the brink of extinction due to the loss of their natural habitats. The intricate balance of ecosystems, cultivated over millennia, is thus disrupted, cascading into the disruption of essential services like water purification, pollination, and soil conservation, which are fundamental to human survival. In combating deforestation, we endeavor not just to preserve trees, but to safeguard the delicate equilibrium that sustains life on Earth for generations to come.

7. Environmental Injustice and Disparities: Environmental injustice and disparities stem from the harsh reality that the burden of environmental degradation falls heaviest on already vulnerable communities, perpetuating a cycle of inequality. These communities, often marginalized by societal, economic, or political forces, face the brunt of pollution, inadequate access to clean water and air, and the consequences of climate change. Consequently, rectifying these disparities isn't just about environmental preservation; it's a fundamental step towards rectifying social inequities and fostering a truly equitable society. Acknowledging and acting upon ecological justice is an indispensable stride toward dismantling systemic discrimination, empowering marginalized voices, and crafting a world where every individual, regardless of their background, can thrive in an environment that nurtures rather than hinders their potential.

8. Sustainable Solutions are Vital: In an era defined by pressing environmental concerns, the imperative for sustainable solutions has become undeniably paramount. As the delicate balance of our planet's ecosystems teeters on the brink, the adoption of forward-thinking practices and cutting-edge technologies has transcended mere preference to become an absolute necessity. By embracing a comprehensive approach that places conservation, renewable energy sources, circular economies, and responsible consumption at its core, we can pave the way for a brighter and greener future. The symbiotic relationship between humanity and the environment calls for a harmonious coexistence, one that recognizes the finite nature of our resources and champions innovative strategies to ensure their longevity. Only through the collective commitment to sustainability can we hope to mitigate the adverse effects of climate change, preserve biodiversity, and secure a thriving world for generations to come.

9. International Cooperation is Essential: In an increasingly interconnected world, the imperative of international cooperation becomes indisputably evident when confronting the pressing issues of our time, particularly those pertaining to the environment. The complex and intricate web of environmental challenges, such as the ominous specter of climate change and the precarious state of endangered species, pay no heed to artificial geopolitical boundaries. Recognizing this, nations are compelled to join hands in a concerted effort to craft and implement collective solutions that transcend individual interests. Global collaboration through international agreements, such as the Paris Agreement, not only acknowledges the shared responsibility for safeguarding the planet's well-being but also harnesses the combined knowledge, resources, and innovation of nations to devise effective strategies. By bridging divides and fostering a united front, international cooperation offers a beacon of hope in the face of ecological adversity, showcasing humanity's potential to rise above differences for the greater good of the Earth and its myriad inhabitants.

10. Individual Actions Matter: Individual actions wield significant power in shaping the world we inhabit. Every person possesses the capacity to enact change by fostering a heightened awareness of their choices and embracing responsible behaviors. By conscientiously opting for sustainable alternatives, such as minimizing carbon emissions and adopting eco-friendly practices, individuals can play a pivotal role in curbing the adverse impacts of climate change. Through these deliberate efforts, we can pave the way for a brighter future, supporting conservation initiatives and fortifying the global mission to preserve our planet's precious ecosystems. The ripple effect of these small yet purposeful steps reverberate far beyond personal spheres, inspiring a collective movement towards a more harmonious coexistence with nature and setting in motion a cascade of positive transformations for generations to come.

Given these undeniable environmental truths, we must act collectively and urgently to safeguard the planet's health and secure a sustainable future for future generations. We can only reverse the negative trends and build a more harmonious relationship with nature through a concerted effort.

While these environmental truths are supported by an overwhelming consensus among scientists, policymakers, and environmental experts, denial and skepticism persist among certain groups and individuals. Environmental denial is the rejection or dismissal of scientific evidence and consensus about the state of the environment and the role of human activities in contributing to environmental problems[33].

Environmental Denial Manifestations

1. Climate Change Denial: Climate change denial stands as a persistent and concerning phenomenon within the realm of environmental discourse. Despite the abundance of compelling scientific data unequivocally linking human activities, notably the combustion of fossil fuels and rampant deforestation, to the profound alterations in Earth's climatic patterns, a faction of individuals and collectives remains steadfast in contesting the veracity of climate change or minimizing its far-reaching implications. This denial not only clashes with the consensus among experts but also hinders meaningful efforts to address the pressing global issue. As the world grapples with escalating temperatures, extreme weather events, and melting ice, the endurance of climate change denial underscores the complex interplay between scientific evidence, personal beliefs, and the imperative for collective action to mitigate the impending environmental challenges that affect us all.

2. Anthropogenic Causation Denial: Anthropogenic causation denial presents a perplexing stance that challenges the prevailing scientific consensus linking human actions to a spectrum of pressing environmental challenges. In the face of widespread agreement among experts that activities such as industrial emissions, urbanization, and resource exploitation are undeniably linked to issues like deteriorating air quality, the fragmentation of habitats, and the alarming decline of biodiversity, a subset of individuals persists in asserting that these predicaments are exclusively the result of natural processes, distinct from any human impact. This denial not only disregards the piles of evidence connecting human actions to environmental degradation but also undermines the urgency for adopting sustainable practices and policies to safeguard the planet's delicate ecological balance. As the tangible consequences of human-induced environmental changes become increasingly evident, acknowledging the intricate interplay between human activities and ecological issues becomes essential for fostering a holistic understanding that can drive effective solutions for a more harmonious coexistence between humanity and the natural world.

3. Environmental Regulation Denial: Environmental Regulation Denial refers to the stance taken by certain groups and individuals who actively contest or undermine the implementation of vital ecological regulations designed to mitigate pollution and safeguard natural resources. Despite the overwhelming scientific consensus underscoring the imperative of these regulations, dissenting parties often advance claims that range from asserting the redundancy of such rules to highlighting the perceived financial burdens or potential hindrances to economic advancement they might impose. This stance, however, dismisses the established link between unchecked pollution and environmental degradation, and disregards the intricate balance required to harmonize economic development with the preservation of our delicate ecosystem.

4. Renewable Energy Skepticism: Renewable Energy Skepticism persists as a counterpoint to the fervent momentum towards adopting sustainable energy solutions in the face of escalating climate concerns. Amidst the global chorus advocating for a paradigm shift to renewable sources aimed at curbing greenhouse gas emissions, a subset of individuals remains entrenched in their reservations about the practicality and viability of these technologies. Their skepticism orbits around a multifaceted uncertainty: whether renewables can satiate the voracious appetite for energy consumption, if they possess the resilience to uphold power grids reliably, and whether their environmental benefits come untarnished by unanticipated repercussions. This cadre of doubters raises poignant questions, casting a probing light on the intricacies and potential shortcomings of the renewable energy narrative, thereby stimulating a discourse that underscores the need for comprehensive understanding and innovative solutions to bridge the chasm between aspiration and implementation.

5. Deflection and Distortion of Facts: Environmental denial goes beyond simply rejecting the existence of environmental problems; it encompasses a range of tactics, including the deflection and distortion of facts. In this strategy, information is manipulated or misinterpreted to minimize the severity of environmental issues or redirect responsibility towards unrelated factors. This insidious approach can give rise to deliberate misinformation campaigns, sowing seeds of confusion and impeding effective action to tackle pressing ecological challenges. By obscuring the truth and altering the narrative, deflection and distortion tactics hinder the collective resolve needed to foster sustainable solutions and safeguard our planet's future.

6. Cherry-Picking Data: Cherry-picking data is a deceptive tactic often employed by denialists, wherein they meticulously select isolated data points or specific studies that align with their preconceived viewpoints, deliberately disregarding the extensive corpus of scientific investigation that refutes their assertions. By cunningly cherry-picking only supportive evidence and turning a blind eye to the broader spectrum of rigorous research that contradicts their stance, denialists craftily construct a distorted narrative that distorts the genuine state of the environment. This calculated manipulation of information not only misleads the public but also undermines the essence of scientific inquiry by sidestepping the holistic and balanced examination crucial for a comprehensive understanding of complex issues.

7. Attacks on Scientists and Experts: In a concerning trend, certain individuals and factions have increasingly turned to the tactic of ad-hominem attacks directed at scientists and experts who courageously voice their concerns about pressing environmental matters or propose essential policy modifications. These attacks, characterized by their personal and often baseless nature, seek to erode the credibility of these knowledgeable figures and cast doubt upon the robustness of scientific consensus. By tarnishing the reputation of these reputable sources, these attacks aim to subvert public faith in the integrity of scientific findings and recommendations, ultimately impeding the momentum for meaningful environmental change. This worrisome phenomenon highlights the broader challenge of safeguarding the crucial role that experts play in guiding society toward a sustainable future and underscores the imperative to promote constructive dialogue rooted in evidence and respect.

8. False Equivalencies: Denialists might draw false equivalencies between different scientific viewpoints, treating fringe or non-peer-reviewed theories as equal to well-established scientific evidence. This tactic can create confusion and give the impression that the scientific community is deeply divided on critical environmental matters.

Despite environmental denial, it is essential to recognize the vast body of scientific research supporting our understanding of environmental challenges. Addressing denial and skepticism is crucial for fostering evidence-based decision-making and implementing practical solutions to safeguard our planet for future generations. To combat denial and promote environmental truths, it is crucial to implement a multi-faceted approach that addresses the root causes of deprivation while encouraging informed decision-making and responsible action[34].

Strategies to Address Environmental Denial

1. Strengthening Scientific Communication: Enhancing the efficacy of scientific communication is paramount, as it entails refining the transmission of intricate research outcomes to the broader public, decision-makers, and vested parties in a manner that is lucid, comprehensible, and captivating. This endeavor necessitates a symbiotic partnership between scientists and adept communication specialists, amalgamating their expertise to adeptly articulate multi-faceted environmental concerns. By sidestepping technical terminology and furnishing information grounded in empirical evidence, this collaborative approach can circumvent the obfuscation of concepts and foster a deeper understanding of critical issues, ultimately empowering society at large to make well-informed decisions and inciting responsive action.

2. Countering Misinformation: In the face of a growing tide of misinformation and disinformation campaigns aimed at eroding the foundation of environmental facts, it is imperative to construct proactive and robust strategies. By instituting fact-checking initiatives that rigorously assess the validity of claims, society can equip itself with accurate information to navigate the complex landscape of environmental issues. In tandem, fostering media literacy through comprehensive educational programs will empower individuals to discern reliable sources from the sea of falsehoods, enabling them to make informed decisions. Establishing symbiotic partnerships with reputable news outlets bolsters the dissemination of truthful narratives, ensuring that a unified front against misinformation is presented. Through these multifaceted approaches, we can effectively combat the dissemination of misleading information, fortify the understanding of environmental realities, and lay the groundwork for a more informed and responsible global citizenry.

3. Promoting Environmental Education: Promoting environmental education is imperative for fostering a sustainable future. By implementing comprehensive environmental education programs spanning from schools to community centers, society can empower individuals with the essential knowledge and critical thinking skills needed to grasp the complexities of environmental issues and their potential solutions. Through these initiatives, students and community members alike will gain a deeper understanding of the intricate interplay between human actions and the natural world, thus cultivating a sense of responsibility and a proactive approach towards preserving our planet. Such education will not only foster environmentally conscious behaviors but also inspire innovative thinking, driving the development of strategies that mitigate ecological problems and pave the way for a more harmonious coexistence between humanity and the environment.

4. Engaging with Diverse Audiences: Engaging with diverse audiences involves a nuanced approach to crafting messages that deeply resonate across a spectrum of demographics, cultures, and belief systems. It necessitates an astute understanding of varied communities, acknowledging their distinct values and priorities. To effectively address environmental issues, it's crucial to re-frame these concerns in manners that seamlessly align with their specific interests and apprehensions. By embracing this strategy, communication transforms into a bridge that transcends differences, fostering a shared commitment to environmental stewardship that encompasses and embraces the rich tapestry of humanity.

5. Fostering Collaboration: Promoting and nurturing collaboration across the diverse spectrum of environmental stakeholders, including scientists, policymakers, businesses, and local communities, emerges as a pivotal strategy in cultivating innovative and sustainable solutions for our pressing ecological challenges. By inclusively engaging all stakeholders in the intricate web of decision-making processes, a harmonious synergy is created that facilitates the seamless translation of knowledge into impactful action. This collaborative approach not only enhances the quality and feasibility of solutions, drawing upon the multidimensional expertise of each group, but also fosters a shared sense of ownership and responsibility in addressing environmental concerns. Ultimately, this holistic engagement paves the way for a more comprehensive and effective approach towards bridging the gap between theory and practice, ushering in an era of transformative change that benefits both our planet and its inhabitants.

6. Incentivising Sustainable Practices: In order to foster a greener and more environmentally conscious society, it is imperative to establish a framework of incentives and policies that promote sustainable behaviors. By offering enticing economic rewards, such as tax benefits for enterprises embracing eco-friendly technologies and financial incentives for individuals actively curbing their carbon emissions, we can catalyze a widespread shift towards responsible practices. These incentives not only bolster the adoption of sustainable solutions across industries, driving innovation and reducing overall environmental impact, but also empower individuals to make conscientious choices in their daily lives. By aligning economic gains with environmental stewardship, we forge a path towards a more sustainable future, where ecological concerns are seamlessly integrated into the fabric of both business strategies and personal decisions, ultimately contributing to the preservation of our planet for generations to come.

7. Promoting Civic Engagement: Promoting Civic Engagement entails fostering a dynamic relationship between citizens and the environment by providing them with the tools and avenues to play an instrumental role in safeguarding their surroundings. This is achieved through a multifaceted approach that encompasses community-based initiatives, inviting individuals to take ownership of their immediate surroundings and drive change at the grassroots level. Simultaneously, offering volunteering opportunities taps into the altruistic spirit of citizens, encouraging them to invest their time and efforts towards meaningful environmental endeavors. By facilitating participation in local and national environmental organizations, individuals can broaden their impact, contributing to broader policy advocacy and collective action for environmental protection. In amalgamating these approaches, civic engagement becomes a pivotal catalyst, empowering citizens not only as environmental stewards but also as advocates for sustainable change, thus fostering a harmonious synergy between human society and the natural world.

8. Addressing Cognitive Dissonance: In the process of tackling cognitive dissonance, it is essential to acknowledge its pivotal role in fueling denial and impeding progress towards change, particularly in the context of environmental issues. This recognition underscores the significance of initiating open dialogues that create a safe space for individuals to articulate their anxieties and apprehensions surrounding pressing environmental challenges. By fostering an environment of genuine understanding and empathy, these conversations serve as a conduit for addressing cognitive dissonance, as individuals' concerns are met with compassionate and informed responses. Through these exchanges, a powerful sense of empowerment takes root, allowing individuals to perceive their role in effecting positive change. This approach not only dismantles the barriers constructed by cognitive dissonance but also cultivates a collective determination to engage actively in the transformative processes required to mitigate environmental threats and secure a sustainable future.

9. Supporting Responsible Media Coverage: Promoting Responsible Media Coverage of environmental matters entails fostering a commitment within media establishments to uphold the principles of precision and equity. This involves equipping journalists with the tools to meticulously assess scientific findings, enabling them to discern nuances and implications accurately. By steering clear of sensationalism and steering towards objectivity, media outlets can thwart the inadvertent propagation of misinformation and ensure that their narratives genuinely reflect the complexities of environmental concerns. By prioritizing accuracy and balance, media professionals can become instrumental in enlightening the public, steering collective awareness towards comprehensive understanding, and encouraging informed actions for a sustainable future.

10. Leading by Example: Leading by example is a pivotal catalyst for widespread sustainable transformation, transcending the boundaries of governments, businesses, and influential leaders. As these entities wholeheartedly embrace eco-friendly practices, they illuminate an inspiring path forward, kindling a collective consciousness that propels others to join the cause. The power of this positive precedent ripples across society, cultivating a cascading effect of mindful choices and responsible actions. Through their demonstrable commitment to sustainability, these trailblazers' beckon forth an era where the harmonious coexistence of progress and planet becomes not just an aspiration, but a lived reality for generations to come.

11. Investing in Research: Investing in research dedicated to understanding and addressing environmental challenges is paramount in our pursuit of a sustainable future. By committing resources to rigorous scientific investigations, we can gain deeper insights into complex issues such as climate change, biodiversity loss, and pollution. Through these endeavors, we not only enhance our comprehension of the urgent problems at hand but also unearth innovative and effective solutions that have the potential to transform our approach to ecological preservation. These research-driven discoveries provide the essential foundation for informed decision-making and policy formulation, lending undeniable credibility to the imperative for environmental action. In the face of skepticism or denial, the weight of empirical evidence and scientific consensus derived from ongoing research can serve as an unassailable counterargument, compelling individuals, industries, and governments to recognize the critical need for comprehensive and immediate ecological interventions.

12. Celebrating Environmental Successes: Celebrating Environmental Successes involves showcasing and lauding the remarkable accomplishments stemming from dedicated environmental initiatives, serving as a compelling reminder of the capacity for positive change through unified efforts. By shining a spotlight on these triumphs, we not only underscore the efficacy of collaborative endeavors but also invigorate a sense of purpose and determination within individuals to join the ranks of change-makers. These celebrations serve as beacons of hope, inspiring wider participation and fostering a shared belief that, collectively, we possess the means to address pressing ecological challenges. Through recognition and commendation of achievements, we nurture a culture of environmental stewardship, propelling a ripple effect of engagement that propels us towards a more sustainable and harmonious future.

By embracing these strategies, we can work towards bridging the gap between scientific knowledge and public understanding, fostering consensus, and collectively address-ing environmental challenges for a sustainable and resilient future.

By acknowledging environmental truths and countering denial, humanity can embark on a transformative journey toward securing the well-being of our planet for generations to come. The pressing need to address environmental challenges has never been more evident, and as a global community, we must unite to safeguard the Earth's resources, ecosystems, and biodiversity.

One of the fundamental truths we must accept is that human activities have significantly impacted the environment. From deforestation to greenhouse gas emissions and the overexploitation of natural resources, we have unintentionally disrupted the delicate balance of our planet's ecosystems. By facing these realities honestly and openly, we can move forward with the collective will to reverse the damage and mitigate further harm.

Taking meaningful steps entails adopting sustainable practices across all aspects of our lives. It involves embracing renewable energy sources, reducing carbon footprints, and promoting conservation efforts worldwide. Businesses, governments, and individuals alike must commit to implementing environmentally responsible strategies to ensure a greener, more sustainable future.

Moreover, countering denial and skepticism about environmental issues is crucial in fostering a sense of urgency and collective action. Raising awareness and engaging in constructive dialogue can bridge the gap between different perspectives and facilitate the adoption of practical solutions. By encouraging open conversations, we can empower communities and decision-makers to work hand in hand, transcending borders and ideologies in the pursuit of environmental preservation.

Embracing these truths extends beyond mere pragmatism;

it embodies a profound moral obligation. As the dominant species on Earth, we have a stewardship responsibility to protect the planet and all its inhabitants. Our actions today will shape the world that future generations inherit, and we cannot let short-term gains jeopardize their ability to thrive.

The consequences of failing to act are dire and far-reaching. Climate change, loss of biodiversity, and resource depletion threaten the environment, human health, social stability, and economic prosperity. By acknowledging these environmental truths, we recognize the intrinsic value of all life and our interconnectedness with the natural world. It is an ethical duty to protect the countless species that share this planet with us and to ensure that future generations inherit a vibrant, diverse, and flourishing Earth.

We can usher in a sustainable and harmonious future through collaborative efforts, scientific innovation, and a collective commitment to change. By acknowledging and acting upon environmental truths, we can forge a path toward preserving the planet's beauty, resilience, and abundance for generations to come. Together, we can leave a legacy of responsible stewardship, ensuring that the Earth remains a nurturing home for all life and a source of wonder and inspiration for centuries ahead.

Chapter Eight:
Seeking Balance and a Path Forward

As we conclude our journey, we'll reflect on the delicate balance between truth and deception, pondering whether absolute truth is attainable or remains an elusive and ever-shifting mirage. In an age dominated by vast amounts of information, we must ask ourselves how society can navigate the complexities of this information overload without succumbing to misinformation and manipulation.

The challenges we face in distinguishing truth from deception are more prevalent today than ever. With the advent of technology and the internet, information spreads rapidly and often need proper verification. Misinformation, intentional acts, and the manipulation of facts can influence public opinion and decision-making, leading to dire consequences for individuals and entire communities.

Pursuing absolute truth may be romantic, as biases,

perspectives, and subjective interpretations often color our understanding of the world. However, acknowledging this limitation doesn't mean we should abandon the quest for truth altogether. Instead, it calls for a more nuanced approach to understanding information and embracing critical thinking.

Critical thinking is a powerful tool in our journey toward discerning truth from deception. Encouraging individuals to analyze information critically, question sources, and evaluate evidence can empower them to make informed judgments. By cultivating a society that values critical thinking, we can enhance our ability to discern reliable information from falsehoods.

Media literacy plays a crucial role in this process. Teaching individuals to be discerning consumers of information allows them to recognize biased narratives, sensationalism, and false claims that might be disguised as legitimate news. Media literacy enables people to navigate the vast sea of information with a discerning eye, fostering a more informed and media-savvy society.

Ethical leadership also plays a vital role in shaping a world where truth prevails over deception. Leaders who prioritize transparency, integrity, and accountability inspire trust among their followers. By leading by example, ethical leaders promote a culture that values truth, encourages open dialogue, and embraces diverse perspectives.

To create a world where truth thrives and deception withers, we must work together to build an ecosystem that promotes critical thinking, media literacy, and ethical leadership. Schools and educational institutions play a central role in nurturing these values among the younger generations. In addition, media organizations and tech platforms can contribute by emphasizing fact-checking, responsible reporting, and algorithmic transparency.

Moreover, we must take responsibility for perpetuating truth or contributing to deception. By being conscious of our biases, actively seeking diverse viewpoints, and fact-checking before sharing information, we can each become agents of truth in a world inundated with information.

In a nutshell, pursuing absolute truth may remain a lofty ideal, but that should not discourage us from striving to uncover and uphold facts supported by evidence and critical thinking. Navigating the complexities of information overload requires a concerted effort to foster critical thinking, media literacy, and ethical leadership. By embracing these principles, we can collectively shape a world where truth shines through, dispelling the shadows of deception and building a more informed, compassionate, and enlightened society for future generations.

In the dynamic and rapidly evolving world we inhabit, the quest for equilibrium and forging a clear path ahead can frequently seem like a daunting endeavor. Amidst the whirlwind of our lives, reconciling the various demands of work, relationships, self-improvement, and self-nurturing becomes an intricate dance that often leaves us feeling swamped and lacking clarity in our journey. Yet, during these moments of uncertainty, the pursuit of balance and a sense of purpose becomes paramount for our overall well-being and fulfillment.

In the hustle and bustle of our fast-paced lives, the first step in attaining balance is recognizing that it is not a static destination but a continual process of adjustments and realignments. Just as a tightrope walker maintains equilibrium by making subtle shifts with each step, so too must we navigate the constant flux of our lives, acknowledging that balance may sometimes elude us temporarily, but that doesn't mean it's unattainable in the long run.

One essential aspect of finding equilibrium is understanding the intricate interplay between our different spheres of life. Recognizing that excelling in one area doesn't have to come at the expense of another, empowers us to seek harmonious integration. For instance, fostering solid relationships can bolster our productivity at work and vice versa. Embracing the idea of work-life integration rather than strict separation can alleviate some of the pressures we feel.

However, societal expectations or self-imposed pressures might hinder the desire to pursue balance. It is vital to recognize that balance is a highly individualized concept. What brings harmony to one person's life may not be the same for another. Hence, instead of comparing ourselves to others, we should reflect on our values, passions, and priorities to chart a unique path that resonates with our authentic selves.

Embracing the journey toward balance and fulfillment also entails acknowledging the significance of self-care and personal growth. Amidst our numerous responsibilities and commitments, we must carve out time to nourish our minds, bodies, and spirits. Self-care is not an indulgence; instead, it is an investment in our overall well-being. Whether through meditation, exercise, creative pursuits, or spending quality time alone, these moments of introspection and relaxation replenish our energies and enable us to cope better with life's challenges.

In our pursuit of balance and direction, it's important to remain adaptable and open to change. Our world is ever-changing, and rigidity can impede our progress. Embracing a growth mindset allows us to view challenges as opportunities for learning and development. While charting a path forward, we might encounter unexpected detours or unanticipated opportunities – it's essential to be receptive to these shifts and embrace them as part of our evolving journey.

Finally, seeking balance should be an act of self-compassion rather than a cause for self-criticism. There will inevitably be times when we stumble or lose our way, but these moments should be seen as part of the natural human experience. Instead of criticizing ourselves for perceived failures, let us show kindness and understanding to ourselves. Through self-compassion, we find the strength to pick ourselves up, reevaluate our course, and continue our quest for balance and fulfillment.

In conclusion, the quest for balance and a path forward is an ongoing and intricate journey. By recognizing its dynamic nature, acknowledging our individuality, prioritizing self-care and personal growth, staying open to change, and practicing self-compassion, we can navigate through the complexities of life and find a sense of equilibrium and purpose that leads to lasting well-being and fulfillment.

Seeking balance is an intricate and meaningful journey,

akin to an artful dance where we gracefully navigate the complexities of life, forging harmony among its diverse facets. This pursuit involves a deep-rooted understanding of ourselves, acknowledging and cherishing our unique needs and aspirations while remaining mindful of the needs and well-being of those around us. It is a delicate symphony, striking the perfect chords between setting boundaries to protect our well-being and being adaptable enough to embrace life's unpredictable changes.

In the pursuit of balance, we embrace the ebb and flow of life, recognizing the symbiotic relationship between giving and receiving. We learn to offer our love, time, and support without losing ourselves while also being open to receiving kindness and support from others. This reciprocity nurtures our bonds, creating a harmonious environment where everyone thrives.

At the heart of balance lies the harmonization of productivity and rest. We understand the significance of dedicating ourselves to meaningful work and endeavors while equally appreciating the value of rest and rejuvenation. By weaving periods of revival into our lives, we maintain the vitality necessary to sustain productivity, prevent burnout, and foster sustainable growth.

Achieving balance demands a profound level of self-awareness. We continually explore our thoughts, emotions, and desires and use this knowledge to make intentional choices that align with our core values and long-term objectives. This process empowers us to stay true to ourselves and focus on what genuinely matters.

Mindfulness plays a crucial role in our pursuit of balance. By cultivating the art of being present in each moment, we savor the joys of life, whether grand or modest, and find solace in times of challenge or uncertainty. Mindfulness allows us to let go of the past's regrets and the anxieties of the future, enabling us to embrace the beauty of the present with clarity and gratitude.

Throughout this journey, we acknowledge that balance is not a fixed destination but a constant evolution. As life unfolds, we adapt our dance, shifting and swaying to maintain equilibrium amid changing circumstances. This flexibility fosters resilience, ensuring we remain steadfast despite the unpredictable tides that life may present.

In conclusion, seeking balance is an ongoing quest to create harmony within us and the world. It requires embracing our individuality while remaining attuned to the inter-connectedness of humanity. This graceful dance demands self-awareness, mindfulness, and intentional choices to synchronize our actions with our deepest values and aspi-rations. As we embrace this pursuit, we nurture a profound sense of fulfillment, living our lives in accord with our true selves and fostering a thriving, balanced existence for both us and those we touch with our presence.

In the contemporary, hyper-connected world we inhabit, it has become increasingly effortless to be overwhelmed and influenced by external forces and the expectations soci-ety places upon us. Amidst the constant flood of messages concerning success, accomplishments, and the definition of a satisfying existence, it is crucial to retain a sense of self and recognize that finding balance is a unique and personal endeavor for everyone. Achieving harmony in our lives necessitates profound introspection and a genuine comprehension of who we are.

With the advent of advanced technology and social media, we are bombarded by a ceaseless stream of information and comparisons. We witness the polished and curated lives of others, which can often lead to feelings of inadequacy and the pursuit of an unrealistic ideal. The pressure to excel in various aspects of life can feel immense, prompting us to strive for accomplishments that might not align with our genuine desires and values.

Nevertheless, amidst this sea of external influences, it is vital to recognize that true fulfillment and balance do not have a uniform definition. What may constitute a fulfilling life for one person might not hold the same meaning for another. The journey to attaining balance requires us to delve deep within ourselves, listen to our innermost thoughts and feelings, and ascertain what resonates with our authentic selves.

It is a process of introspection wherein we explore our passions, dreams, strengths, weaknesses, and the values that underpin our character. By undertaking this inner quest, we gain a clearer understanding of our aspirations and what genuinely brings us joy and contentment.

In the pursuit of balance, we must also learn to distinguish between our desires and the expectations imposed upon us by external sources, be it society, family, or friends. While some external guidance can be constructive, we should not allow it to overshadow our innate sense of purpose. Embracing our individuality and being true to ourselves empowers us to forge a path that aligns with our aspirations and values.

We might encounter obstacles and uncertainties in this profoundly personal expedition toward balance. Nonetheless, these challenges present opportunities for growth and self-discovery. With resilience and courage, we can navigate through the complexities of life, uncovering the unique balance that enriches our sense of well-being and contentment.

In conclusion, in today's fast-paced and interconnected world, external influences and societal expectations make it easy to be swayed. However, it is crucial to remember that balance is not a one-size-fits-all concept. It is an individual journey that necessitates introspection and a profound understanding of ourselves. We can cultivate a sense of fulfillment and harmony by embracing our authenticity and pursuing a path aligned with our inner aspirations and values. This inner journey towards balance grants us the strength and resilience to face life's challenges gracefully and purpose, ultimately leading to a more gratifying and meaningful existence.

Finding balance begins with self-reflection, a profound journey of introspection that allows us to delve into the depths of our being. This transformative process involves setting aside moments of serenity and contemplation, granting ourselves the invaluable gift of self-awareness.

During this inward exploration, we carefully examine our priorities, recognizing what truly holds significance in our lives. We question the sources of our motivations, whether they stem from societal expectations, external pressures, or our genuine desires. By unearthing these fundamental truths, we liberate ourselves from the shackles of conformity, discovering the essence of our authentic selves.

As we traverse this path of self-discovery, we scrutinize our values, seeking to understand the principles that under-pin our choices and actions. We question the origins of these beliefs and whether they genuinely resonate with our inner compass. This process grants us clarity and empowers us to embrace values that align with our core identity, fostering a profound sense of coherence and integrity.

Moreover, finding balance necessitates a thorough eval-uation of our goals. We delve into the aspirations that drive us forward and examine whether they reflect our deepest yearnings or are merely superficial desires. Through this examination, we refine our goals, allowing them to evolve with our evolving selves and ensuring they serve as beacons guiding us toward authentic fulfillment.

Amidst this profound introspection, we acknowledge the facets of life that bring us joy and fulfillment. Whether pursu-ing creative passions, nurturing meaningful relationships, or engaging in acts of service, we unearth the wellsprings of contentment unique to each of us. Recognizing these sources of joy, we embrace them wholeheartedly, and in doing so, we infuse our existence with purpose and genuine satisfaction.

With newfound self-awareness, we can make informed decisions that align with our authentic selves. The fog of uncertainty dissipates, and we confidently chart our course, knowing that each step we take resonates with our deep-est aspirations. We no longer squander our time and energy on endeavors incongruent with our identity but channel our resources towards meaningful pursuits, amplifying our sense of purpose and personal fulfillment.

In conclusion, finding balance is a profound and reflective expedition. It involves peering into the recesses of our being to understand our priorities, values, and goals. Engaging in this transformative process clarifies what truly matters to us, paving the way for a harmonious existence that exudes authenticity and genuine happiness.

Moreover, seeking balance is an intricate journey that demands us to embrace the art of setting boundaries in various aspects of our lives. It's about finding equilibrium amidst our daily demands and responsibilities. Understanding the significance of limitations can foster a healthier and more fulfilling existence. Learning to say "no" becomes essential in this pursuit of balance. While it may seem uncomfortable or even challenging, saying "no" enables us to protect our time and energy from being depleted by excessive commitments or activities that don't align with our priorities. By respectfully declining requests or opportunities that don't resonate with our goals, we free ourselves to focus on what truly matters, allowing us to be more present and effective in those areas.

In this journey towards balance, we also acknowledge the significance of creating space for activities and relationships that nourish our souls and bring joy. We recognize that dedicating time to hobbies, passions, and meaningful connections enriches our well-being. By prioritizing these aspects, we infuse our lives with positivity, creativity, and inspiration, contributing to a more harmonious existence.

Furthermore, part of setting boundaries involves

recognizing our limits as human beings. We come to terms with the fact that we are not invincible, and we need moments of rest, relaxation, and self-care to replenish ourselves physically, emotionally, and mentally. By honoring these needs and taking the time to rejuvenate, we prevent burnout and maintain a sustainable pace in our endeavors.

Setting boundaries also plays a significant role in protecting our mental and emotional health. When we establish limits on what we allow into our lives, such as toxic relationships or negative influences, we create a safe space for personal growth and self-improvement. This environment fosters a positive mindset and confidently empowers us to pursue our goals and aspirations.

Setting boundaries cultivates a nurturing atmosphere for our well-being and personal development. It allows us to preserve our energy, focus on what truly matters, and foster meaningful connections. By asserting ourselves and communicating our limits effectively, we create an environment conducive to balance and growth, promoting a life aligned with our values and aspirations.

In conclusion, embracing and setting boundaries is essential for those seeking balance. Saying "no" when necessary and making room for activities and relationships that nourish us are vital aspects of this journey. By recognizing our limits and honoring our need for rest and self-care, we safeguard our well-being and establish a foundation for personal growth and fulfillment. Setting boundaries empowers us to create a balanced, thriving life that aligns with our most authentic selves.

In life's journey, we often hear about the importance of balance, and rightly so, as it is the cornerstone of a fulfilling and harmonious existence. However, it's essential to recognize that life is not static; it is a dynamic and ever-changing flow like a meandering river finding its course through diverse landscapes. As we navigate this dynamic flow, seeking balance becomes an art of continuous adaptation and growth.

Pursuing balance is not a destination with a fixed endpoint; instead, it is an ongoing process that requires us to be open-minded and flexible. Just as the tides ebb and flow, we must be willing to adjust our sails and redefine our paths when needed. This adaptability is a mark of resilience and strength, allowing us to face the challenges that life presents gracefully.

In the pursuit of balance, we must cultivate self-awareness and self-compassion. We should not be too hard on ourselves when we encounter moments of imbalance or feel overwhelmed. It is normal to experience periods of intense focus on specific aspects of life while temporarily neglecting others. Instead of dwelling on perceived failures, we should remind ourselves that it's all part of the journey.

Patience is another crucial virtue in the quest for balance. As we strive to create equilibrium among the various dimensions of our lives, we must acknowledge that achieving perfect balance all the time is unrealistic. There will be moments when certain areas of our lives require more attention, whether personal growth, career development, relationships, or health. Embracing the natural ebb and flow of life's demands allows us to grow and evolve at our own pace.

Learning is an integral part of the journey toward balance. We gain wisdom and insight from both our successes and setbacks. Every experience teaches us something valuable. Instead of viewing failures as roadblocks, we can see them as opportunities for growth. When we encounter challenges, we can learn valuable lessons that shape our future decisions and actions, ultimately contributing to a more balanced and fulfilling life.

Moreover, balance is not a solitary endeavour; it involves our interactions with the world and the people around us. Cultivating meaningful connections with others and nurturing positive relationships can contribute significantly to our sense of balance and well-being. We can learn from others' experiences, share insights, and support one another in our journeys.

In conclusion, while balance is a fundamental aspect of a fulfilling life, it is essential to recognize that life is not static but fluid and ever evolving. Embracing the journey toward balance requires adaptability, self-compassion, patience, and a willingness to learn and grow. As we continue this path, let us remain open to change, celebrate our progress, and be kind to ourselves during moments of imbalance. Remember that the pursuit of balance is not a destination but a lifelong expedition towards a more harmonious and enriched existence.

In our quest for balance and a meaningful path forward, we can find tremendous benefit in seeking support from others. The journey towards self-discovery and growth can often feel overwhelming, but connecting with like-minded individuals is a powerful way to ease the burden and gain fresh perspectives.

Engaging with those who share similar goals and aspirations creates an environment of understanding and empathy. Such connections offer a sense of belonging, knowing we are not alone in our struggles and aspirations. In these communities, we can freely express our thoughts and emotions, fostering a more profound camaraderie that empowers us to overcome challenges together.

In addition to seeking peer support, reaching out to mentors or professionals can be transformative. With their wisdom and experience, mentors can offer valuable guidance, helping us navigate obstacles and avoid potential pitfalls. Their insights shed light on aspects of our journey that we might have overlooked, allowing us to make more informed decisions.

Likewise, professionals who are experts in their respective fields can provide specialized knowledge and strategies tailored to our unique situations. Whether it's a life coach, career counselor, or therapist, these individuals can offer valuable tools and techniques to help us find the balance and direction we seek.

Surrounding ourselves with a supportive community is essential for personal growth. This network of individuals uplifts and motivates us, providing a safe space to share our struggles, fears, and aspirations without judgment. Through open and honest conversations, we gain clarity on our goals and values, enabling us to make choices aligned with our true selves.

As we confide in trusted individuals, we may realize that many of our struggles and fears are shared experiences. This realization brings comfort and strengthens our determination to overcome challenges. It becomes apparent that growth is not a solitary endeavor, but a collective effort fueled by the encouragement and support of those around us.

In conclusion, seeking support from others is a valuable and empowering step in finding balance and forging a meaningful path forward. Connecting with like-minded individuals, seeking guidance from mentors or professionals, and embracing the strength of a supportive community offer us a wealth of insights, encouragement, and clarity. Together, we can navigate the complexities of life, face our fears, and strive toward a brighter and more fulfilling future.

Ultimately, seeking balance and a path forward is a profound and intimate journey with the potential for transformation and growth. It is a voyage of self-discovery, exploring our innermost desires and acknowledging our vulnerabilities. This pursuit demands a genuine commitment to ourselves – a dedication to explore deep into the recesses of our minds and hearts.

The first step on this path is self-reflection, the art of looking inward to understand who we are, what drives us, and what truly matters to us. It requires courage to confront our fears, insecurities, and past experiences and the wisdom to embrace our strengths and unique qualities. Through self-reflection, we can clarify our purpose, aspirations, and the things that bring us joy and fulfillment.

Yet, this journey is not just about seeking answers but also about nurturing ourselves along the way. Self-care becomes an essential aspect of this transformational expedition. It means prioritizing our physical and mental well-being and recognizing that taking care of ourselves is not selfish but necessary. By nurturing our bodies, minds, and spirits, we become better equipped to face challenges and embrace life's opportunities.

As we embark on this quest, we must extend self-compassion towards ourselves. Accepting that we are imperfect and prone to mistakes and setbacks is fundamental to growth. Being kind to ourselves in moments of failure or disappointment allows us to learn from our experiences and move forward with resilience. Self-compassion nurtures a positive relationship with us, promoting a sense of acceptance and love that enables us to be more compassionate toward others.

Finding balance in life is not a linear process. The journey may present twists, turns, and uncertainties. But by staying open to each twist's lessons, we can gradually uncover the harmony we seek. It involves making intentional choices – aligning our actions with our values and passions. This requires discernment, knowing when to say "yes" to opportunities that align with our vision and when to say "no" to those that do not serve our well-being.

As we embrace this transformative expedition, we craft a life that truly honors our authentic selves. By nurturing our passions and prioritizing what truly matters to us, we have a uniquely fulfilling and purposeful path. Each step forward becomes a deliberate stride towards a life that resonates with our deepest desires and values.

In essence, seeking balance and forging a meaningful path is not an end goal but an ongoing process of growth and discovery. This adventure allows us to live authentically, with integrity and wholeheartedness. By cultivating self-aware-ness, self-care, and self-compassion, we can walk this path with grace and embrace the inherent beauty of the journey itself. Along the way, we may inspire others to embark on their voyage of self-discovery, creating a ripple effect of posi-tive transformation in the world.

Epilogue:
Embracing The Light

The world was at a precarious crossroads in the wake of relentless battles between shadows and illumination. The relentless struggle between truth and deception had taken its toll on humanity, leaving scars on hearts and minds that seemed indelible. The quest for knowledge and understanding had transformed into a high-stakes endeavor, where the line between fact and fiction blurred, and reality appeared to be merely an illusion.

But amidst the chaos and confusion, a resilient spirit emerged. People from all walks of life realized the significance of seeking truth and embracing the light of knowledge. The world witnessed a remarkable awakening as individuals sought to break free from the shackles of misinformation and deceit that had permeated their lives for far too long.

It was a period of profound introspection when societies

questioned the very foundations upon which they were built. Institutions that once held absolute authority were now scrutinized, and accountability became the rallying cry. Armed with courage and determination, truth-seekers united to dismantle the walls of deception that had kept them apart for so many years.

As the shadows began to recede, a newfound sense of unity and empathy spread across the globe. The barriers that had long divided nations and peoples began to crumble, and a global consciousness emerged. No longer confined to the narratives spun by those in power, the masses found their voice, empowered to challenge the status quo and demand transparency.

The advent of technology played a pivotal role in this awakening. The digital age, which had initially allowed misinformation to spread like wildfire, transformed into a formidable weapon against deceit. Innovative platforms emerged, designed to fact-check information, promote critical thinking, and encourage responsible knowledge-sharing. The power of social media, once used to manipulate and divide, became a catalyst for constructive dialogue and collective action.

By recognizing the irreversible shift in the zeitgeist, governments and leaders began to prioritize transparency and accountability. Leaders who had once thrived on deception found themselves increasingly isolated as the masses yearned for honesty and authenticity. The paradigm shifted, and those who chose the path of truth and integrity garnered respect and support from their constituents.

However, the struggle was far from over. The forces of deception, though weakened, continued to linger, seeking new ways to sow discord and confusion. The battle between shadows and illumination had evolved into a perpetual dance, an ongoing quest for balance in a world where truth was revered and threatened.

Education emerged as the cornerstone of a progressive society in this new era. Schools and universities redoubled their efforts to foster critical thinking and information literacy. Armed with knowledge and empathy, the youth became the torchbearers of truth, challenging the old order and paving the way for a brighter future.

The epilogue of this ongoing saga needs to be addressed. The struggle between truth and deception persists, weaving its way through the tapestry of human history. But the lessons learned from the battles of yesteryear have left an indelible mark on the collective consciousness. The quest for truth and the pursuit of light are now embedded in the very fabric of human existence.

As we move forward, let us remember that the struggle between shadows and illumination is not confined to ideas but manifests in our everyday actions. Let us be the champions of truth, embracing empathy and understanding as we navigate the complexities of our interconnected world, for it is in the relentless pursuit of reality that we shall find the path to a more enlightened and harmonious future.

Notes

1. Nakano, R., Takanashi, T., Surlykke, A., Skals, N., & Ishikawa, Y. (2013). Evolution of deceptive and true courtship songs in moths. *Scientific Reports*, *3*(1), 2003.
2. Griffith, R. L., & McDaniel, M. (2006). The nature of deception and applicant faking behavior. *A closer examination of applicant faking behavior*, 1-19.
3. McGlone, M. S., & Knapp, M. L. (2019). Historical perspectives on the study of lying and deception. *The Palgrave handbook of deceptive communication*, 3-28.
4. Hyman, R. (1989). The psychology of deception. *Annual review of psychology*, *40*(1), 133-154.
5. Yuill, J., Denning, D., & Feer, F. (2007, January). Psychological vulnerabilities to deception, for use in computer security. In *DoD Cyber Crime Conference* (Vol. 2007).

6. Dixon, P. (2002). Political skills or lying and manipulation? The choreography of the Northern Ireland peace process. *Political studies, 50*(4), 725-741.

7. Collett, T. S. (1993). Disclosure, Discretion, or Deception: The Estate Planner's Ethical Dilemma from a Unilateral Confidence. *Real Prop. Prob. & Tr. J., 28*, 683.

8. Ho, S. M., Hancock, J. T., & Booth, C. (2017). Ethical dilemma: Deception dynamics in computer-mediated group communication. *Journal of the Association for Information Science and Technology, 68*(12), 2729-2742

9. McAuliffe, D. (2005). I'm still standing: Impacts and consequences of ethical dilemmas for social workers in direct practice. *Journal of social work values and ethics, 2*(1), 1-10.

10. Deshai, N., & Bhaskara Rao, B. (2023). Unmasking deception: a CNN and adaptive PSO approach to detecting fake online reviews. *Soft Computing*, 1-22.

11. Cortright, D. (Ed.). (2020). *Truth Seekers: Voices of Peace and Nonviolence from Gandhi to Pope Francis.* Orbis Books.

12. Boghossian, P. (2002). The Socratic method (or, having a right to get stoned). *Teaching Philosophy, 25*(4), 345-359.

13. Finocchiaro, M. A. (2012). *Galileo and the art of reasoning: Rhetorical foundation of logic and scientific method* (Vol. 61). Springer Science & Business Media.

14. Mandela, N. (2008). *Long walk to freedom: The autobiography of Nelson Mandela.* Hachette UK.

15. Phillips, M. (2011). *The world turned upside down: the global battle over god, truth, and power.* Encounter Books.

16. Lewandowsky, S., Ecker, U. K., & Cook, J. (2017). Beyond misinformation: Understanding and coping with the "post-truth" era. *Journal of applied research in memory and cognition*, 6(4), 353-369.
17. Khaldarova, I., & Pantti, M. (2016). Fake news: The narrative battle over the Ukrainian conflict. *Journalism practice*, 10(7), 891-901.
18. Pariser, E. (2011). *The filter bubble: What the Internet is hiding from you*. penguin UK.
19. Cinelli, M., De Francisci Morales, G., Galeazzi, A., Quattrociocchi, W., & Starnini, M. (2021). The echo chamber effect on social media. *Proceedings of the National Academy of Sciences*, 118(9), e2023301118.
20. Pérez-Escoda, A., Pedrero-Esteban, L. M., Rubio-Romero, J., & Jiménez-Narros, C. (2021). Fake news reaching young people on social networks: Distrust challenging media literacy. *Publications*, 9(2), 24.
21. Prior, M. (2013). Media and political polarization. *Annual Review of Political Science*, 16, 101-127.
22. Fallis, D. (2014). The varieties of disinformation. *The philosophy of information quality*, 135-161.
23. Sukardi, R. A. Q. S. (2015). Machiavellian Principles Depicted in William Shakespeare's Othello. *Lexicon*, 4(2), 145-152.
24. Tsikerdekis, M., & Zeadally, S. (2014). Online deception in social media. *Communications of the ACM*, 57(9), 72-80.
25. Covacio, S. (2003). Misinformation: Understanding the evolution of deception. *Informing Science, June*.

26. Crilley, K. (2001, September). Information warfare: new battle fields Terrorists, propaganda and the Internet

27. Oswald, M. E., & Grosjean, S. (2004). Confirmation bias. *Cognitive illusions: A handbook on fallacies and biases in thinking, judgement and memory, 79.*

28. Arthur, C. (2014). *Digital wars: Apple, Google, Microsoft and the battle for the Internet.* Kogan Page Publishers.

29. Rubin, E. L. (2016). Rejecting Climate Change. *Journal of Land Use & Environmental Law, 32*(1), 103-150.

30. Grušovnik, T. (2012). Environmental denial: why we fail to change our environmentally damaging practices. *Synthesis philosophica, 27*(1), 91-106.

31. Rubin, E. L. (2016). Rejecting Climate Change. *Journal of Land Use & Environmental Law, 32*(1), 103-150.

32. Tollefson, J. (2019). The hard truths of climate change--by the numbers. *Nature, 573*(7774), 324-328.

33. Wyatt, T., & Brisman, A. (2017). The role of denial in the 'Theft of Nature': Comparing biopiracy and climate change. *Critical Criminology, 25*, 325-341.

34. Wong-Parodi, G., & Feygina, I. (2020). Understanding and countering the motivated roots of climate change denial. *Current Opinion in Environmental Sustainability, 42*, 60-64.

Acknowledgments

In diving into the intricate interplay between truth and deception, and in the pursuit of unveiling the shadows and illumination that define our world, I owe my deepest gratitude to those who have been instrumental in shaping this endeavour.

Foremost among these individuals is uncle late, Thel Mou Akeen Mou, whose profound insightful song and unwavering commitment to the pursuit of truth have been a constant source of inspiration for me. Your dedication to shedding light on the complexities of our reality and your passion for uncovering the veils of deception have motivated me to embark on this journey of exploration.

I extend my heartfelt appreciation to my mentor, whose guidance and wisdom have been indispensable throughout this expedition. Your support in encouraging me to question conventional wisdom and to seek knowledge beyond the surface has been transformative for both my research and my personal growth.

To my beloved family and friends, your unconditional love and unyielding belief in my abilities have been the bedrock of my perseverance and determination. Your encouragement has fueled my passion to navigate the intricacies of this subject matter and seek a deeper understanding of the world's struggle between truth and deception.

I would also like to acknowledge my peers and colleagues, whose stimulating intellectual exchanges and constructive feedback have enriched this project.

Lastly, I am indebted to all the researchers, authors, and scholars whose prior work has paved the way for this study. Your contributions have set the stage for progress and innovation in the field of unveiling truth and deception.

To each person mentioned above and, most notably, to late Thel Mou Akeen Mou, whose inspiration has been a guiding light, I express my heartfelt gratitude. Your influence has shaped not only this book but also the person I have become on this path of exploration.

With sincere appreciation and a renewed commitment to seeking truth, Gabriel Garang Pioth.

About the Author

I n the book, *"Shadows and Illuminution: Unveiling the World Struggle between Truth and Deception,"* we follow the captivating journey of Gabriel Garang Pioth, a Medical Laboratory Scientist who is wholly consumed by his relentless pursuit of truth. Driven by an insatiable thirst for knowledge, Gabriel's scientific background and literary creations intertwine to reveal how the struggle between truth and deception had left indelible scars on the hearts and minds of humanity. The quest for knowledge and understanding had transformed into a high-stakes endeavour, where the line between fact and fiction are blurred, and reality appeared to be merely an illusion. But amidst the chaos and confusion, a resilient spirit emerged. People from all walks of life witnessed a remarkable awakening as individuals sought to break free from the shackles of misinformation and deceit that had permeated their lives for far too long. Institutions that once held absolute authority were now scrutinized, and accountability became the rallying cry. Armed with courage and determination, truth-seekers united to dismantle the walls of deception that had kept them apart for decades. As the shadows began to recede, a newfound sense of unity and empathy spread across the globe. The barriers that had long divided nations and peoples began to crumble, and a global consciousness emerged. No longer confined to the narratives spun by those in power, the masses found their voice, empowered to challenge the status quo and demand transparency. The advent of technology which had initially allowed misinformation to spread like wildfire transformed it into a formidable weapon against deceit. Innovative platforms emerged, designed to fact-check information, promote critical thinking, and encourage responsible knowledge-sharing. The power of social media, once used to manipulate and divide, became a catalyst for constructive dialogue and collective action. The truth has finally triumphed over deception!

Appendices

U ncle Thel Mou Aken Mou's poignant composition dives into the eternal battle between truth and deception, capturing the essence of this timeless conflict through the haunting melody and evocative lyrics. With a masterful blend of emotive and soul-stirring vocals, the song paints a vivid sonic landscape that mirrors the intricate struggle between honesty and deceit. Through its resonant verses, Uncle Thel Mou Aken Mou invites listeners to reflect on the complexities of discerning reality from illusion, making this musical creation a profound exploration of human experience. The theme of the song is universal. The song was composed in Dinka (see Appendix A), and translated into English (see Appendix B).

Appendix A: Waa Thel Muön Akëën ë Mɔ̈u

Thel Muön Akëën ë Mɔ̈u
Thöc aa baa rou

Alë yïïyoo ku thöc aa baa rou!?
Thöcdït cë kɔc këëk aa baa rou!?
Thönydïït wäär lueel Arab kek ë Muɔnyjäŋ aloi ë rot
Ku thöny ë lueth kek yic kïn
Ka cïï lueth kɔc göök thïn
Yee ŋa bë kënë lueth jal piŋ
Bë lac lueel?

Naa week ë bäny muk biith
Ku bäny ë galaam
Ku bäny kɔ̈k acɔ̈ɔr ë Nhialic
Yee ŋa bë kënë lueth jal piŋ
Bë lac lueel?

Mën cïï lueth ka yic waar ë thööc nhom
Bë yaa lueth yenë bëny ë baai
Ku lueth acath kek ë yɔ̈ɔm rac apɛi:

Acath kek ë guöpdhääl
Ku acath kek ë nyinriɛl wär peeth
Ku acath kek aa tuöör ë nyin
Ku acath kek aliääp
Ku acath kek ë Tiɛɛl-Majɔŋdït

Ku acath kek ë luɔɔm ku kookdït
Ku acath kek ë kɔɔc juääc kɔk cää ben lueel

Naa cɔk aa banykuun ë luök luk
Kaa laŋ yiic kɔɔc cë kënë lueth gam
Bäny kɔk ë luök dool aa tɔu thïn
Ku kaa kɔɔc akut ë lueth ë path

Dömdöm ë lueth kek ë thööc
Yen acïï piny maan
Be rot kaŋ jɔt ë ruöön wäär
Bë kɔc duër wäl wei
Naa wënë buk jal gäi
Kadït cë röt looi
Kë yee piny la lëëklëëk!

Goo lueth ke raan tooc
Ku bïï ku lueel alä kee dhäldhäl
Yenë piny met bë la lëëklëëk
Goku jäl thiëc
Dhäldhäl cäk tïŋ
Yee tik ka yee moc
Agoo nhom ciën këdeen ben lueel?
Ka baa raan akut ë lueth ë path

Këc kë tïŋ ka benë lueel
Alë kee Majaŋ-Adɔɔr?
Ku aa kɔɔc wäär
Cïï kaken tuöör nyïïn

Ku bïk döŋ kek ë mɛɛm
Naa wënë lök keek liëm thook ë kɔɔc ë duɔɔl
Ka pël ë ke riɛnken
Rin ë kɔɔc cë mam
Ku ye lueel
alë kee Majaŋ-Adɔɔr

Ku yee wën ë ŋa kë cɔl adɔɔr
Kuëndïït-Aguɔɔk ku Agar e Wöl?
Naa wiëckë wun ë lueel yeen
Ka bäk wïc
Ku abäk yök ka cɔl raan akut ë lueth ë path

Kadït cë röt looi alɔŋ daan ë Junub
Kë lee ɣook pën thoŋ yee kɔc jam kek ë Nhialic
Acït awuöc ku awuöc

Awuöc arëër kek ë Nhialinydïït ë pan ë Junub
Jɔŋ rɛɛc cë wël tuööm kööth
Bë kɔc röt maan na cɔk aŋɛk kek ë manh ë man
Kaa bë röt dhiɛl nɔk ë thoŋ cïï luum lueel
Naa cɔk aa wëldït cë mat ë thuɔŋ tök yic
Kaa ŋuɔt ë ka rɛc Magɔkdït ë lum

Acëŋ ë Raan-Macär yee ŋö loi rot?
Yee ŋö bee yïn kɔc cak ba luum cɔl ajuëc
Ku cɔl alueth ajuëc
Ku yɔ̈ɔ̈m ë raan dïït puöu
Ku mëtiɛl-apeth

Kaa keek aa juëc baai
Ku cɔl atëët alik pandaan ë Junub
Ku bä atëët yaa cɔl aye tök ku rou?

Acëŋ ë Deŋ-Macärdït yïn ajör ɣook
Acëŋ ë Deŋ yïn aŋuɔt yïn jör ɣook
Nhialiny Abuŋ ë Deŋ yïn aŋuɔt yïn jör ɣook

Ka yeen naa wïc ba ɣook kony?
Ka yïn cɔl Deŋ cath kek ë yic adöt ɣook
Ku dhuök ë alueth ciëën

Deŋdïït wäär yen cath kek ë yic
Ku thaabuun juëc
Bë puön ë Muɔnyjäŋ lɔɔk ebën
Ku wel thok abak
Ku ben puön ë Nuëër lɔɔk
Ku wel thok abak
Ku cɔl ala tueny Door ku Jurcol yic
Ba cɔl ajuak atëët yiic pandaan ë Junub
Ku dhuökë alueth ciëën

Nyaaië lum
ku dhuökë alueth ciëën
Ku nyaaië mëtiɛl-apeth
Ku dhuökë alueth ciëën
Ku cɔl atët aye dhiëth atët
Ku duk cɔl aben wääc pandaan ë Junub
Ka yïn acë kɔc dööt

Ka yïn acë kɔc dööt
Ku abuk lueel alë ɣääië wää!
Ka yïn acë kɔc dööt
Ku abuk lueel alë ɣääi!

Ku naa yee yic yen muk thööc
ŋuöt ë Gäräŋ ë Mabiör akëc thou
Ku döŋ Umer Bacïïr?

Ku bënydït Kiir ë Mayär akïn
Aŋuɔt ë buöc kek ë kuat ë jɔk thɛɛr wäär ë wïïn cuet
Naa cë ɣɔk lony bïk la nyuëth
Ka jɔk lök wïïn cuet

Ku të ye kuöny wïïn aba lëk week
Mïthkuaan ë Junub
Wïïn aaye kuany bë keek rek
Ku wïn ë thɔn
Aye kuany bë nöök ë ɣoro nhom
Naa cɔk jöŋ yaa tïŋ
Ka cïï kɔŋ dööt
Duäkë wïn ë Kiir
Cɔl aben jöŋ cuet

Nhialiny ë kɔɔc col abë guɔ ɣëët
Mïthkuaan ë Junub
Yakë röt theek ebën ebën ebën ebën
Ku nhiarkä raan duön tööŋ laŋ thok yic
Ku nhiarkä Thälpa Kiir ë Mayär bënydaan ë Junub
Dɛɛt ë yï puöu yïn abïï Nhialic dööt.

Appendix B: Song of Thel Mou Aken Mou

Thel Mou Aken Mou
Oh! Behold there are two seats!

Oh! behold there are two seats!
The great seats of controversy are two!
The seat that was contested by the Arabs
and the Muonyjang is separate
But the seat of lie and the truth is here usurped by the lie

Who can reveal the machination of the lie
and promptly say it?
How about you spear masters, the scholars,
and other masters who pray to God?
Who can reveal the machination of the lie
and promptly say it?

Now the lie has replaced the truth
to be the leader of the land
And lie is accompanied by a nasty entourage:
It's accompanied by disrespect
It's accompanied by sorcery-surpassing impulsiveness
It's accompanied by chaos
It's accompanied by demonic jealousy
It's accompanied by gossiping
And gluttony the great

It's accompanied by numerous other people
whom I do not want to mention
Even among your leaders who hear court cases
Are those who have accepted the machination of lie
There are leaders who complicate court cases
But they belong to the organization of lie

The seat captured by the lie
Is the reason the earth was angry last year
That it nearly tip the people off
And when we wondered why these big miracles occurred!
Why the earth was quaking?

Then the lie sent someone
Who came and said
That it was an earthquake
Then we asked him:
Is an earthquake a man or a woman?
But he lacked what to say
He was just a member of the organization of lie

You see
It's also said that it's an emaciated Majak
But these are the people
Whose properties were looted
And left vulnerable
When fed by the international community
Their names as the vulnerable people were scrapped
And referred to instead as an emaciated Majak.

And whose son is called Emaciated,
Kuendit of Aguook and of Agar e Wol?
If you are searching for the owner of this false missive
You shall search
But you will find out that he is called
a member of the organization of lie

Having been denied the language of speaking with God
is a big thing that has happened in our country, Junub
It looks like an error but it's indeed an error
An error is with the great God of Junub

A devil has messed things up
Causing hatred amongst the people
Even brothers from one mother
Will kill each other
Because of the word coming from the gossiper
Even profound verbal agreements
Can be dismantled by the gossiper

What's happening, creator of the black race?
Why did you create people
Such that gossipers are numerous,
And liars are numerous
All kinds of greedy people
And sorcerer-jealous people
Are numerous in the land
And artisans are few in our land of Junub
Such that artisans are counted one or two?

Creator of nimbus cloud rain
You're mistreating us
Creator of rain
You are mistreating us
God of Abuk of rain
You're mistreating us

If you want to help us
Let the rain that is accompanied by the truth come to us
And take back the liars
The rain that was accompanied by the truth
And many soaps
To wash the entire heart of the Muonyjang
And turns it in one direction
And then washes the heart of Nuer
And turns it in one direction

And let it rain in Door and Jurcol lands
To increase the number of artisans in our land of Junub
And take back the lairs
Have the gossipers
And take back the lairs
Have the sorcerer-jealous
And take back the liars
And let an artisan procreate an artisan
And let it not go wrong again
In our land of Junub
And you would have redeemed the people
And you would have redeemed the people

And we would sigh — aaiwaa
And you would have redeemed the people
And we would sigh — aaai

And if the truth had the seat
Then Garang e Mabior
Would not have died and
Left Omar Bashir behind

And here is the great leader, Kiir Mayar
Still struggling with tethering-leath
rope-eating dogs of long ago
Who when the cows are released to the pastures
The dogs would eat the tethering leather ropes
Sons of Junub, I will tell you
how to protect the tethering ropes
The tethering ropes are looped together
And the masculine tethering rope
is hanged on the branch rack
And the dog would not reach even though it sees it
Don't let the dog again eat Kiir's tethering rope
The God of the black race will arrive soon
Respect one another
All all all all of you
And love the only one of you who still speaks the truth
And love Salva Kiir Mayar
Our leader of Junub
Strengthen your heart
God will come to your aid